A SHOT RANG OUT . . .

Just as Johnson's gun leveled off, a single shot rang out. A spot of red appeared on the outlaw's shirt, and the man dropped to his knees. The gun fell from Johnson's fingers and his eyes became cloudy.

I ran over beside Fletcher. We walked together to where Johnson lay.

"Who . . . are . . . you?" Johnson gasped as the blood poured forth from the hole in his chest.

"Some call me Fletcher," Fletcher said.

"No," Johnson said, looking at him with confusion. "Something else. On the Cimarron. I saw you. You . . ."

But Johnson spoke no more than that. His eyes went blank, and he toppled over face down in the dusty street.

WEST OF THE CIMARRON

BY SPUR-AWARD WINNING AUTHOR
G. CLIFTON WISLER

ZEBRA BOOKS
KENSINGTON PUBLISHING CORP.

ZEBRA BOOKS

are published by

Kensington Publishing Corp.
475 Park Avenue South
New York, NY 10016

First printing: October 1985

Printed in the United States of America

I

The warm summer breeze swept across the broad grassland, stirring the buffalo grass so that it seemed to be an ocean of yellow blazing in the afternoon sunlight. For a hundred miles this yellow sea was broken only here and there by a small white farmhouse, a barn, a thread of fenceline or the tell-tale tracks of the Atchison, Topeka and Santa Fe rail line. Soon it would be part of the new state of Colorado. For now there was only a rare cavalry outpost and an occasional territorial marshal to represent the ever-encroaching arm of civilization.

There was a town there, named after a railroad surveyor called Whitlow who'd been paid for his work with a tract of land. Mr. Whitlow had long since left the country, leaving only his name and a small telegraph office behind as a reminder that he'd passed that way.

The town had grown without him. Now there was a brick bank building, a church and a school. A cluster of stores and two saloons spread out from the little square that would one day hold a courthouse. And the railroad depot was the finest east of Pueblo.

Whitlow's people were a quiet, God-fearing bunch.

5

They tended their own business and left everybody else to do the same. But if a neighbor had a need, he rarely had to ask for help. It was a fine place to live to raise children, to grow up.

In those days you could still put yourself on the back of a horse and ride off down the road past the last fence. Sometimes buffalo herds would still graze there. Every once in a while a band of Comanches or Kiowas would wander by to the southwest, and Cheyennes sometimes camped to the north.

Some of the people who lived in town could remember when Indian villages hugged the banks of the Cimarron River east of town. A few had come over the old Santa Fe Trail in covered wagons years before. Most had come lately, though, settling where their fare money took them on the rail line.

Our place was about a mile out of town. My father had brought my mother there the year after the war against the Yankees. They were from Texas, and it'd been a long trip. I was born in a little town called Jacksboro back in Texas, but we'd come to Whitlow when I was a baby, and I didn't remember anything about Texas.

That summer I was twelve years old. It had been a hard year, a year full of pain and growing and tragedy. In the midst of that ocean of prairie, I stood on a small hillside beside a delicate white picket fence. Inside the fence was a small clearing about five square yards in area. In the middle of the clearing stood three identical white wooden crosses.

The two oldest ones were marked with the names of my little brother Michael and my baby sister Elsa. They had died during a bad winter four years before. The third cross, the one with the fresh coat of white paint, carried the name of my father. He'd only been thirty-five years old. It didn't seem fair that he should be gone.

I took my small hand and ran it along the length of the splintery fence. My mind ran back to the time four years before when we'd built it.

"Michael loved to ride with me out to the hills," my father had said. "We saw some buffalo out there once. He wanted to ride one of them."

My father had laughed. It was the first time in weeks his face had been bright.

"He was just like you, Eric," Papa had said. "He wanted to know everything. He wanted to do everything. He never cried, even when he was really sick. He'd like the hill, don't you think?"

"I guess," I remembered saying. Back then I hadn't understood much about dying. I only knew our room was kind of empty without Michael running around.

Reverend Manchester had come from town to read over Michael and Elsa. He'd said some pretty words about children. I wish I could remember them. They made me feel better.

We didn't put them in a wooden box like they put Papa in. We wrapped Elsa in her pretty baby dress. Mama carried her and laid her in the ground.

Papa carried Michael. My brother Tom and I had put him in his favorite quilted blanket that morning. Michael's face was still, frozen, and his little hand was cold to touch. It had scared me.

"The earth is warm," Papa had said. "Let it keep those who are dear to us."

Mama had cried. Tom and I had stood stiff, trying to be brave like Papa had said. My four-year-old brother Willie had clung to my side. Willie didn't understand where Michael had gone. I didn't either.

About a week later we started building the little picket fence. Papa got hold of some pickets cheap down at the depot. Some lady in town had ordered

7

them for her house, but she died before they arrived. Papa paid the shipping charges and hauled the pickets out to the hill in our wagon.

"This will kind of set this hill aside for Michael and Elsa," Papa said. "It will kind of be our special place."

"Our place?" I remembered asking him.

"Sure, Eric," he told me. "There's a price for anything. The first men who settled these parts fought the Indians to claim this ground as their own."

"Who do we fight?" I had asked.

"We fight nature," he said. "We fight the cold, the heat, the drought. Our family paid for this land with two of our own. You remember the story your mama told you about her grandfather, Will Delamer?"

"The one who came to Texas when it was still part of Mexico?" I asked.

"That's the one. He came originally with his father from France. They took the name De la Mer."

"It means from the sea. I remember," I'd told him.

"Do you remember what he told your grandfather when he went off to fight in the war for independence?"

"No," I said, sighing.

"He said that in order to be free, men pay terrible prices. He told all about how their family had been mistreated in France. When they came to America, they put all the letters together, Delamer. Now they would be Americans, free."

"His son is the one who died in the war," I said.

"That's right. Your uncles, two of them, fought in the war against the North, too. Your Uncle Sam was a captain. He came home to find the Comanches had burned everything. His father had died in the war. His mother died of the cholera. What did he do? He

8

started building all over again. One day you'll meet him, shake his hand."

"The other brother died, didn't he?" I asked Papa.

"I don't know," Papa said, rubbing his chin the way he did whenever he wasn't sure of something. "I think your mama got a letter from him one time. He's the one we named Willie after. Your mama always liked him best, I think."

"And I have another uncle in Texas. He's a lawyer."

"That's James," Papa said. "He's the one who writes you on your birthdays."

"They're all Delamers. How come I don't have any uncles who are Sheidlers like you and me?"

"None of my brothers ever lived past childhood, Eric," Papa had said, sitting down beside the partially completed picket fence. "They died like Michael, swept away by the cold almost before they had a chance at life."

"I miss Michael, Papa," I said.

"Me, too," he said, putting that great huge hand of his on my small shoulder. "But we men have to be tough. We have to face up to things."

"Why'd Michael have to go away?" I asked.

"Sometimes there are no whys, Eric," he said. "There are no reasons for things being the way they are. We just have to understand we can't change what happens. We can only try to make it easier to live with."

"Like building a fence up here?" I asked.

"Yes," he said, smiling. "Maybe we can plant some flowers. Elsa liked flowers."

"When I die, I want to be up here, too," I said.

"That won't be happening for a long, long time," Papa told me. "You've got too much life in you to be thinking about death."

I remembered thinking that Michael had been

pretty lively, too. I wanted to ask him more about Michael and about me and about life, but I saw his eyes grow strange. It was like he was far away, and I started hammering the pickets again.

We didn't have all that many times alone together. Most of the time Tom was along, and Papa never liked to talk about serious things when Tom or Willie was there. Tom was only a year younger than me, but he never seemed to worry about things like I did.

Papa wanted to make sure we never had food problems, so he gave up depending on the farm for all our money. We still kept cows and had a nice garden, but he quit planting corn and wheat. Instead he bought a piece of land in town and decided to open a feed and grain store to supply the other farms and ranches.

Papa used all the money he'd saved to buy lumber for the place. Then one day he loaded Tom and me into the wagon, and we headed into town. I was barely ten, hardly big enough to help. Tom really couldn't help at all, but Papa brought him along to fetch water and bring nails. It was really to let Tom know he counted, too.

Papa was a carpenter by trade. I never saw a man who could do with wood the things he could. In one day he had the floor laid out. It took us the better part of the next week to get all the planks nailed down, though.

As I worked at his side, there was a special feeling of closeness between us.

"This is a better way to trim the planking, Eric," he'd say, then show me how. "You can do that faster this way," he'd tell me a little later.

Papa never told me I was stupid or that I was doing something wrong. It was always that there was a better way or had I forgotten this tip or that. I don't suppose I helped very much, but I felt that store had part of me in it. As the walls were framed and the roof put on, we looked at it with great pride.

"One day your kids will run through that store, and you'll tell them about how you and their grandfather built it," Papa said as we put the windows in.

I remember hooking my arm around him and squeezing him tightly. He lifted Tom in one arm and me in the other and held us up for everybody to see. I never felt prouder than when he let me know I belonged to him.

When I was eleven, I got bit by a rattlesnake. Papa cut my leg open and sucked out the poison. Then when the chills came, he wrapped me in a blanket next to the fire and stayed up all night with me. I remember him talking to Mama about it.

"He won't die," Papa said. "There's a God in heaven, and He knows I've felt too much pain in my life. He took two brothers from my arms when I wasn't as big as Eric. He took Michael and Elsa away. He won't take Eric. That boy's my heart."

I remember Mama sat down with him and put her arm around his powerful shoulders.

"He's a strong little boy," she said. "He's tougher than he looks. He could get himself bitten by ten snakes and be running through the fields by Sunday."

Papa had been worried, though. Every hour or so he'd feel my head and frown.

"Fight it, Eric," he said. "If you see that ugly old grim reaper coming for you, fight him. Tell him your papa's got need of you yet. Tell him you're a Sheidler, a fighter."

The doctor came from town to look at me after three days. He said the fever should've broken. Likely I'd die. Papa almost threw him out of the house on his seat. Sure enough, by Sunday I was chasing Willie

11

around the barn.

I never told him, but I figure it was Papa's prayers that kept me around. Rattlesnakes kill a lot of kids as small as I was. That summer we rode out and shot about twenty snakes to get back at them for biting me. It was pretty poor revenge. Snakes just bite to be natural. But nobody's been bitten around our place since.

"Papa, I miss you," I said to him, fingering the side of the fence.

Then I stepped away from the little graveyard and frowned. A tear wove its way across my cheek, falling to the ground below. A second formed in my eye, but I brushed it away.

"I'll get them, Papa," I said, gritting my teeth. "I'll make them pay."

Then I took out his Colt revolver and ran my fingers along the cold barrel.

II

The ride back to the house was less than a mile, but in my sadness it took half an hour. When I got to the barn, I slid off the back of the big sorrel and led him to the watering trough.

"Have a good drink, boy," I told the horse. "Good horse," I said, stroking his nose.

I remembered Papa saying I was good with horses.

"That Eric was born to work with horses," Papa said one time to a friend of his. "When he's older, we should send him out to spend a summer on his uncle's ranch. Sam raises some top notch horses, you know."

I thought many times about how wonderful it would be to spend a summer with my mysterious Uncle Sam on his ranch down on the Brazos River in Texas. It would be fun to run through the river with my cousins, hear all the stories about my famous grandfather, Big Bill Delamer, the first white man to live in that part of the country.

Now that would never happen. The day Papa was buried I became a man. Now I'd stay on the ranch. When I was old enough, I'd make those men pay for killing Papa. Tom and Willie could go to Uncle Sam. I could not.

As I brushed the sorrel, the two black mares whinnied at me from their stalls. Tom hadn't brought them their water. They'd have to be put out in the pasture to graze, too. It wasn't like Tom to neglect his work. You could usually count on him to take care of things.

"Tom!" I cried out. "Tom?"

"That you, Eric?" my brother yelled out from the house. "You there, Eric?"

"Here," I said, walking out the barn door. "How come you didn't put the horses out to graze?"

"Eric," my brother said, running to my side. "Eric, we've been looking all over for you. I even sent Willie to town."

"What's the matter?" I asked.

"It's Mama, Eric. She's not feeling good again. Only this time she looks pretty bad. I think maybe she's dying."

"Oh, she is not," I said. "She's just down with something. You get those horses out to the pasture and let them graze some. I'll see to Mama. And don't ever send Willie to town by himself. You know the way those men act. They're liable to shoot him or something."

"Not even Dunstan would shoot an eight-year-old kid," Tom said.

"Why not?" I asked. "He had Papa killed. I heard he shot a couple of kids not much older than me down on the Cimarron during the range wars."

"No kidding?" Tom asked.

14

"You've seen him, haven't you? He's a cold blooded killer."

"Maybe I should ride into town and get Willie," Tom said. "He's awful small to get himself shot."

"What're you going to ride?" I asked. "You haven't fed the horses. I just got off mine. No, you get the horses to pasture. Willie'll be all right. Nobody knows him in town. They just know me. They wouldn't mess with him. He stays out of people's way."

"What if they ask where you are?" Tom asked.

"Yeah," I said, frowning. "He'd better be all right, Tom. He's Mama's favorite."

"I'm sorry, Eric," Tom said, looking up at me. "I just didn't know what to do. Mama was calling for you, and I couldn't find you. I didn't know what else to do."

"It's all right," I said. "Take care of the horses."

"Sure, Eric," Tom said to me.

I trotted to the house and walked inside. The house was always warm in the summer, even when a breeze came from the mountains. Only the rains cooled things off, and there hadn't been any rain for more than a week.

"Mama?" I called out. "Are you in bed?"

"Eric?" she called feebly to me. "Where have you been?"

I walked in and sat down on the side of her bed.

"Eric, I feel a fever coming on," she said.

I took my hand and pressed it against her forehead. She took it in her soft hand and kissed it.

"Your head's a little hot," I said. "Do you need anything?"

"Yes," she said frowning.

15

Looking into her sad eyes, I knew what she was thinking.

"I've been to see him," I said. "I just stood there beside the crosses and remembered him. Mama, I miss him so."

"I know, Eric," she said. "It's been hardest on you."

"It's all right," I said. "I can take it. I just have to get bigger pretty fast."

"You're big right now," she said, smiling in a far off sort of way. "Eric, I'm so dizzy this afternoon. The boys will be hungry. Do you think you can manage something for them to eat?"

"Sure," I said.

"Eric, is there anything left in the garden? I haven't tended it properly. The planting is behind. There's always so much to do."

"Don't worry, Mama," I said. "Everything will be fine."

"Are you sure, son? It seems to me everything is confused."

"Mama, you just rest now," I told her. "Tom and I can get things taken care of. I talked to Mr. Franks about butchering a cow. He said he'd pay us for some of the meat. We'd have fresh meat for almost a week."

"Thank God for the cattle. And the chickens. We always have eggs and milk. But the vegetables. We need them, too. Your papa hunted to get us through the winter. I wish he'd taken you last year. You might be able to shoot a deer."

"I could shoot a deer," I said. "I could even shoot a man."

"Don't ever talk like that in my house," she said. "Haven't you seen enough death in your young life?"

"Yes, ma'am," I said. "But it's the wrong people who've died."

"There's never a right person where death is concerned," she said. "Everybody is somebody's father or brother or husband."

"Yes, ma'am," I said.

"Now get busy and find us something for dinner," she said, kissing my hand again. "Eric, you make quite a man."

"Thanks, Mama," I said, running out of the room.

When I got to the garden, Willie came walking up the road. I waved at him, and he ran to me.

"Eric, I went to town to find you," he said.

"I'm here," I said, patting him on the shoulder like Papa did to me when I was little. "Did you have any trouble in town?"

"No," he said. "Eric, that man's still there. You know."

"Tripp Hunt?" I asked.

"Yeah," he said. "The one who . . ."

"I remember what he did," I said. "As soon as I get big enough, bam! He'll be dead."

My face was full of anger, and Willie stepped away from me.

"Your face is scary, Eric," he said, frowning. "When you talk like that, you scare me. Tom, too. He says you're going to shoot that man. Eric, that man shoots good. He might shoot you."

"Nobody's going to shoot me," I said. "It's going to take practice, but I'll get to where I'm faster than all of them."

"Couldn't you just send them away, Eric? Maybe Mama can send for Uncle Sam. I'll bet he'd know what to do."

"We don't need anybody, Willie. Now go inside and sit with Mama. I'm going to get some vegetables from the garden."

"But, Eric," Willie said, "there hasn't been anything in the garden for a week."

"Make sure you don't say that to Mama," I said. "Swear it, Willie."

"Okay," he said, his bright eyes full of confusion. "I swear. But Mama's going to find out sooner or later."

"Later's always better than now," I said. "Now get going."

As Willie disappeared from sight, I walked out past the barn to the fields. There I knelt down and began digging wild turnips. They had little taste, and there was never a feeling of satisfaction after eating them, but added to the little wild onions that grew in the fields, too, they could make a meal.

"I wish I had a few potatoes," I whispered to myself. "Or some dried beef. It would make a good meal."

But there were only the onions and turnips. I filled my hat with them, then walked back to the house.

"What's for dinner?" Tom asked me as I approached the house.

"What else?" I said.

"Not turnips again," he said sourly. "Eric, I'm going to turn into a turnip."

"We have some eggs," I said.

"We eat eggs for breakfast," Tom said. "How do we eat them, boiled or raw?"

"Onion and turnip soup," I said.

18

"The horses aren't the only ones that're going to be hungry," Tom said, making a face. "Eric, can't we maybe sneak into town and see if Mr. Grant at the mercantile has a little extra candy?"

"Mr. Grant doesn't run the mercantile anymore, remember?" I said. "Now help me get dinner."

"Sure," he said, following me.

We boiled the vegetables and pitched in some scraps of carrots. Then I salted and peppered the soup and waited for it to start boiling.

At dinner I got only blank looks from my brothers. They weren't exactly mad, but they sure weren't happy.

"I hate turnips," Willie said finally, setting his spoon down. "I never want to see another turnip."

"The Indians lived off wild turnips," I said. "They'd have starved without them."

"Well, no wonder they got themselves wiped out," Willie said. "They probably didn't even mind."

"Don't talk stupid," I said. "Turnips are good for you."

"Eric, what're we going to do?" Tom asked. "Mama's going to notice the turnips, too. She's going to figure it all out."

"We're going to slaughter one of the cows tomorrow," I said. "Turnips and onions will taste fine in stew or on the side with steaks. I talked with some of the neighbors about getting some potatoes. I'm going to mend some fences."

"I'll help," Tom said.

"You will not," I told him. "Look, Tom, if Mama finds out, she'll have a fit. Besides, there's too much for you to do here. The horses and the cows and the chickens. Those chickens keep us

19

going, you know."

"I know," Tom said, frowning.

"I'd better go see how Mama is," I told them.
Then I emptied my bowl of soup and walked to
Mama's room.

"Eric, the soup was a little . . . a little . . ."

"I'm sorry, Mama," I said, sitting on the edge
of her bed like always. "I'm not much of a cook."

"It's hard to make much out of wild turnips,"
she said. "How long has the garden been empty?"

"A week," I said, looking away from her. "I'm
sorry, Mama. I didn't know when to plant everything. You always did that. I've tried to keep
things going, but . . ."

"I know you have, Eric," she said. "You're
doing just fine. I should be more help."

"You're sick," I said.

"Not that sick," she said. "It's just that we were
doing so well. Your father had the store going in
town. We didn't think we'd have to farm anymore.
And now . . ."

"Mama, we'll make out," I said. "We'll have the
cattle, and I talked to some of the neighbors
about vegetables."

"I'll not have you taking charity," she said.

"Not charity," I said. "We're trading for them."

"Trading what?" she asked.

"Different things," I said.

"What, Eric?" she asked. "Tell me this minute."

"I'm going to mend some fence, Mama," I told
her. "I know you don't like me working for other
people, but I have to check our fences anyway, so
. . ."

"I guess it was bound to happen," she said. "I
don't like it, Eric. You have enough to keep you

20

usy here."

"What?" I asked. "Tom can tend the stock. Mama, we have to do what we can to get by."

"I know," she said. "I'll show you how to fix the turnips, too. That's about all we had to eat when we first got here. You and Tom were practically weaned on turnips."

"Tom and Willie don't much like them, Mama," I told her. "Turnips are kind of tasteless."

"They sure beat starvation," she said, managing a small smile. "Now there's something else I wanted to talk to you about."

"Yes, ma'am," I said.

"I noticed this afternoon that your father's pistol is gone from the gun rack. Do you know where it's gotten to?"

"I have it," I said quietly.

"Why, Eric?" she asked. "Boys shouldn't play with handguns."

"I'm not a boy anymore," I said. "I should have had Papa around to teach me how to shoot it. Instead I have to teach myself. I'm all we've got to defend us."

"Defend us?" she asked. "Is that why you took it? A Winchester rifle is for defending. A pistol's only good for killing a man. You plan on killing someone. And we both know who."

"What do you expect?" I asked. "I can still remember that man standing over Papa, laughing at him. I see his eyes, and I want to blow that man's head right off."

"Eric, you've got to let him go," she said. "We all miss him. You're going to have enough to keep you busy without worrying about killing a man."

"Mama, you can't expect me to forget," I said.

21

"Look at us. We're digging in the ground for wild turnips to eat. Our store, the place Papa and built with our own hands, was taken away from us. I'll never forget."

"I'm sorry you feel that way, Eric," she said sadly. "Maybe you're too young to understand what I'm trying to tell you. I've seen hate destroy good men. Maybe you'll be lucky enough to grow out of it."

"Mama, I won't do anything until I'm sure. But when I'm fast enough, quick as lightning, then they're going to be dead."

"Or you will," she said.

I looked into the sadness written all over her face. Then I took her empty bowl back to the kitchen and helped Tom clean up.

III

That night I sat up for a long time cleaning Papa's Colt revolver. I wanted to go out behind the barn and shoot at old bottles, but the sound would surely be heard by Mama. Mama wasn't feeling very well that night, and I didn't want her worrying about me.

The house was still hot that night. Evening usually brought a cool breeze through the windows of my room, but the air was deathly still that night. As I undressed, I looked over at my brothers.

Willie was lying there like always, his eyes closed, the moonlight dancing across his bright face. I pulled the sheet over his bare shoulders and smoothed out a strand of his golden hair. Every time I looked at Willie sleeping alone in the bed beside mine I remembered how Michael's bright little face had once smiled at me from beside Willie.

Too much sadness had filled my life. I sat down on the edge of my bed and pulled off my shirt. Throwing it on top of my trousers, I whispered my prayers.

"And God," I said, finishing up. "Look after us,

God, help me out. Don't let anything else happen to us. Watch out for Mama, God. She's all we'v got left."

I swallowed the tear that wanted to come. Then slid into bed and pulled my share of the sheet over me. Tom stirred a moment, but he didn't wake up He slept like a log, and there was never any danger of waking him up, getting into bed.

We'd thought a couple of times of putting another bed in the room for Tom. Tom suggested maybe he and Willie share one bed. But Willie always objected.

"That's Michael's place," Willie told us.

It had been four years, but I don't suppose any of us were willing to admit Michael wouldn't come back. And I guess Tom and I figured the day we put the third bed in was the day I'd be really grown up. That scared Tom, and I suppose it scared me, too.

I had trouble sleeping that night. I just lay there staring at the ceiling for hours. Tom was sleeping soundly next to me, but his peaceful slumber wasn't contagious.

When my eyes finally did close, it wasn't peace that came to me at all. I found myself sitting on the little wooden bench Papa had made for me outside the store in town. Papa was inside stocking shelves with a new supply of grain seed.

I sat there whistling the way I used to. I always felt happy in those days. Mama used to say my dark blue eyes were brighter than a summer sky, and my hair was already beginning to be streaked with strands the color of straw. By the summer's end my hair would be as blond as Willie's.

For a moment my mind seemed to wander. I thought about how different I seemed now. My eyes were never clear anymore. Dark circles formed under my eyes most of the time. I never whistled and rarely smiled.

I didn't know Tripp Hunt very well back then. He was a young man in his late twenties. He had a long thick black moustache that curled down around his mouth, and his brown eyes had a wicked quality about them.

He was a flashy dresser. He wore a blue shirt that day with a black vest studded with silver coins. His boots were hand-tooled with fancy three-headed dragons, and he wore a fancy kerchief around his neck.

He had a dozen fine leather hats. That day he wore one that was black as night. It had a white band with a small mockingbird feather in the side.

"Hi, boy," he said to me as he walked up the steps to the store. "Your daddy around?"

"In the store like always," I told him.

"Say, you interested in making a quarter?" he asked. "I could sure use someone to pick up a telegram for me."

"No thanks," I said. "I don't work for strangers."

"You'd do better for yourself losing that attitude, son. You might find I'm a man to know in this town," he said.

"I know everybody I want to know in this town," I told him, frowning. Then I scampered inside the store ahead of him.

"Papa," I said, grabbing his arm. "There's a man here."

"Slow down, Eric," Papa said. "Who?"

"Figure the boy might be talking about me," Hunt said, walking into the store. "Believe we have a bit of business to transact."

"You need some seed, sir?" Papa asked. "Don't have the look of a farmer about you."

"No, Sheidler, my line's a bit more basic. I go in for a different kind of planting, if you catch my drift," Hunt said, flashing his deadly eyes in my direction.

"Make your pitch, Hunt," Papa said.

"You want the boy here?" Hunt asked, pointing at me.

"He's my son. Whatever you have to say to me, you can say to him, too," Papa told Hunt.

"Well, whatever you say," Hunt said. "My words come from Dunstan. He says he likes the banking business. He likes stores too. Like the mercantile. He's really doing a fine business there. He's got a saloon, too. Seems like he'd like to have a feed store now, too."

"Well, I wish him luck. Eric, how long did it take us to get this place going?" Papa asked, pulling me toward him.

"Best part of a year," I said. "And we knew the people."

"You like to make it tough, don't you?" Hunt asked. "My man Dunstan isn't talking about starting his own place. He wants this store right here. He's not interested in taking it for nothing. He figures maybe a hundred dollars would be a fair price."

"A hundred dollars?" Papa asked. "Why, I've put more money than that into stock this week. This store's inventory's worth at least ten times that. I figure the place ought to go for four thousand dollars."

"Think again," Hunt said. "Mr. Dunstan's making you an offer you can't refuse."

"I don't see that at all," Papa said.

26

"Well, let me make my point another way," Hunt said. "There's no orphanage around these parts. A kid without a daddy could starve real easy. Think about that," Hunt added, slapping his holster. "Think real hard. I'll be waiting for your answer."

"You have my answer," Papa said.

"You think some more. Take all the time you need, as long as you make up your mind in ten minutes," Hunt said, laughing. "Ten minutes."

Hunt walked outside and lit a cigar. I turned to Papa.

"What's going on?" I asked. "What's he mean about being an orphan?"

"Get my gunbelt, Eric," Papa said. "Then get out of here."

"I'm not going anywhere," I said, handing him his gunbelt.

"Son, you see that man out there?" Papa asked. "He's smoking a cigar right now. In a few minutes one of us will be dead. Have you ever seen a man killed?"

"No, sir," I said, shaking.

"I don't want you here," he said, putting his hand on my shoulder.

"You never sent me away before," I said, leaning against him. "Not now, Papa."

"Son, this isn't something you understand," he said.

"Isn't it just like what you told me when we worked on the picket fence? Isn't it fighting for our freedom?"

"Yes, son, it is," he told me. "Exactly. I'm no gunman, though, Eric. It could be me lying on the floor in a few minutes."

"No," I said. "That can't happen."

"Eric, you know you've always been special to

27

me. You're stronger than your brothers. You're so little, but I guess it doesn't matter so much a man's size as what he's made of. Take care of your mother if something happens. Now if you have to stay, get over behind that shelf. Now!"

"Yes, sir," I said, scrambling over behind a shelf as Hunt walked back into the store.

"Well, I see you've made your decision," Hunt said, pointing to the revolver my father wore on his hip.

"Cut the talk, Hunt," Papa said.

"You're making a fool's play, Sheidler," Hunt said. "One way or the other this store's going to be Dunstan's. The way I see it, you'd be better off walking out of here. You've got a family to look after."

"I'm not a man to run away with my tail between my legs, Hunt," Papa said. "I'm not afraid of you."

"I know," Hunt said, laughing. "You should be. There's a lot of brave men that die young. You ready?"

"Make your play," Papa said.

It was the last thing Papa ever said. By the time Papa had his pistol in his hand Hunt had fired a bullet into his chest. Papa tottered for a second. He looked at me with a sort of helpless stare. Then his eyes clouded over, and he hit the floor.

I sprang out from behind the shelf, and Hunt turned toward me. His gun swung in my direction, and I froze. Terror gripped me, and my face grew white.

"You?" he asked, cracking a smile. "I thought it was a man," he said, laughing. He laughed and laughed and laughed.

I ran past him and cradled my father's head in

28

my lap. Blood already soaked his shirt, and his eyes were empty. The softness, the goodness was gone. I was all alone.

Looking up at Hunt, I saw him laughing even then.

"He was a fool," the man said. "He got himself killed for nothing."

As his face became distorted in my memory, I sat up in bed, sweating all over. I wanted to scream out, but I had no voice. I was shaking.

"Papa?" I said at last, reaching out for him. But there was no one there to touch.

"Eric, what's wrong?" Tom asked, grabbing my arm.

"Tom?" I asked, trying to shake away the terror.

"You having a nightmare?" my brother asked me.

"Yes," I said, trembling.

"Hey, you're really shaking. I never saw you like this," he said to me.

"It was Papa," I said, sliding my legs over the side of the bed and turning my back to Tom. "I saw it all over again. Hunt, the gun, all of it."

"I miss him, too," Tom said, putting his hand on my shoulder. "But I have somebody to lean on. You don't."

"Somebody to lean on?" I asked.

"You," he said, leaning on me. "I know we've got to act tough, Eric, but I'm scared. I don't show it to Willie, but I'm real worried. What happens when we've eaten all the cows? We can't plant fields, not alone. I don't even know how to grow carrots. And that man Hunt, and Dunstan, and all the rest of them are still in town."

"We'll get by," I told him.

"You sure, Eric?" Tom asked. "Really sure?"

"Yeah," I said. "We have to. When you have to get by, you do it. Mama told me today she and Papa didn't have anything to eat but onions and turnips when they first came here. We can get by on that if we have to."

"But what about Mama?" Tom asked. "I've never seen her so sick."

"It's Papa," I said. "She's lonely. I try to help, but I'm not Papa. If only they'd waited a couple of years. We'd have showed that Hunt, Papa and me. They could never have done that to the two of us."

"Eric, they say Hunt's killed twenty men," Tom said.

"He won't kill people forever," I said. "One of these days it's going to be him lying on the floor. I'll be standing over him, spitting in his face."

"Eric, he's a killer. You couldn't hurt anybody."

"If I'd had a gun in the store, I'd have shot him right there, Tom. I'd have shot him on the spot."

"Would you?" he asked.

"Yes," I said.

"Eric, do you have Papa's pistol?" Tom asked.

"Yes," I told him.

"When you go to shoot it, take me," Tom said. "I want you to show me. I have to know, too. If you . . . if you don't shoot him, then it'll be my turn."

I turned and looked into my brother's eyes.

"Tom, I'm scared of him. I have nightmares. I feel like I'm going to wet my trousers when I walk by him. I hate him so much. I think about all the things I'm going to do to him. I remember hearing Mr. Roderick talk about what the Cheyennes did to captives. I want to do all those things to Hunt. I want to hear him scream. I want to see him beg for mercy. I want to see him dead."

"I don't care about him," Tom said. "Eric, I just wish everything was the way it used to be. I wish they'd just get on their horses and ride away."

"They won't, though," I said. "They'll stay. And one of us will die. No matter what, I won't leave Papa and Elsa and Michael on that hill all alone. I'll stay."

"Then I'll stay, too," Tom said. "Brothers stick together, right?"

"Sure," I said. "We'll stick together."

Tom patted my back, and I managed a smile. Then we both sank back into the comfort of our bed and fell asleep.

IV

Morning broke early across the eastern horizon. As the first golden rays of sunlight swept through the room, I was yawning away the final trace of weariness brought to me by a sleepless night. Leaving Tom and Willie to sleep a little longer, I got into my clothes and tiptoed into Mama's room to check on her.

She was tossing to and fro in her bed. I walked over and touched her head. It was feverish.

"Mama," I said, shaking her shoulder lightly.

"Yes," she said, turning her head toward mine. "Eric, is something the matter?"

"Mama, your head's hot," I said. "I'm going to bring you a wet cloth. Is that all right?"

"That would be just fine," she said.

I walked into the kitchen and pumped a basin full of cool well water. Then I soaked a rag, wrung it out and carried it into her room.

"Here," I said, placing the rag on her forehead. "You'll feel better now."

"Has Tom gone out for the eggs yet?" Mama asked. "There's breakfast to be readied."

"I let him sleep awhile," I said. "We were up late."

"Boys need their sleep," she said. "But not during chore time. You have to force Tom to do his part."

"Mama, Tom works hard. You can always count on Tom. I just wanted . . ."

"You can't shield him from the hardness," she told me. "Your father never did that. He never kept you from things. Eric, you shouldn't do that for Tom. It's not a favor you're doing him. The earlier a boy understands the difficulties of life out here, the stronger he becomes. Only the strong survive."

"Willie, too?" I asked.

"You can let Willie sleep a little later, play a little longer, but he should do his part, too, Eric. I had three brothers. You've heard me talk of them. Sam was always the strongest. My papa included him in everything. My second brother, Willie, was different. He never took interest in the ranch. He spent a whole summer living with the Indians, hunting buffalo and living in a tepee."

"He didn't grow up strong, huh?" I asked.

"He wasn't weak, Eric. He just never belonged to anything. After the war Sam had some place to come home to. Willie just wandered. I used to hear from him. He was in Abilene, then up in Wyoming for a while. Then the letters quit coming. Eric, he was the brightest, most sensitive person I ever knew. He should have had a better life. You remind me of him, with just enough of Sam and your papa thrown in to make you belong."

"I like to hear you talk that way," I told her. "I miss Papa talking about me. He was always saying things about the family, about what I'd grow up to be. Lately I've been so confused about everything."

She took my hand and kissed it lightly the way she did lately when I visited her. I bent over and kissed her cheek.

"Go get Tom moving," she said. "Get me up to fix breakfast."

"Mama, I can cook breakfast," I told her. "I'm good at scrambling eggs. Willie even say so. Maybe you'll feel well enough to fix supper."

"Sure, Eric," she said. "Now be off."

"Yes, ma'am," I said.

I walked back to my room and tapped Tom on the shoulder.

"Time for chores," I said, shaking him.

"All right," he said, moaning. "You ruined a perfect dream. The chickens could've waited."

"Come on, little brother," I said, pulling the sheet off him.

"Who's calling who little?" Tom asked, jumping on my back. "I'm almost as tall as you are."

"Cut it out, Tom," I said, pinning him to the bed. "Get to the barn and get the eggs. I've got things to get done."

"Sure, Eric," he said, stepping away. His eyes had the hurt look in them that came whenever anybody said something rough to him.

"Hey, don't frown like that," I said. "How'd you like to meet me this afternoon down at the creek? We could go swimming."

"That would feel good on a day like this," he said.

"Bring the horses down to graze. Willie, too. I'll be mending fences over at Mr. Hazard's place."

"You want some help?" Tom asked.

"Sure, but you've got chores to do. There's wood to be chopped, the water barrel to fill, and all the animals need to be seen to. You might go down and make sure the cows have plenty of grass. We'll have to move them soon."

"Well, I'd better get the eggs," Tom said. "Mama

34

will be ready to cook them pretty soon."

"Mama won't be cooking breakfast," I said. "I'll get the skillet ready."

"Eric," Tom said, taking my arm and holding me still. "Mama's going to be all right, isn't she?"

"Sure," I said. "I figure she'll be up and around by supper."

"Good," he said, smiling.

I left Tom to get dressed and walked into the kitchen to get everything ready for breakfast. In no time at all we were eating the scrambled eggs.

Mama told me the eggs were good. Willie and Tom ate double what they usually did, probably to make up for the turnip soup the night before. Then we all scattered to our chores.

When I had finished checking and mending Mr. Hazard's fences, I rode by the Hazard's house and told Mr. Hazard.

"Fine, boy," Mr. Hazard said. "It's mighty hot out there today, huh?"

"Yes, sir," I said, wiping the sweat from my forehead.

"Ma's got a sack of potatoes for you. Some carrots thrown in. Figure that's fair, don't you?"

"More than fair, sir," I said.

Mrs. Hazard carried the sack out to me, and I threw it across my saddle horn.

"Thanks, ma'am," I said. "Mama sends her best."

"Thank her," Mrs. Hazard said. "How're the boys?"

"Waiting on me up at the creek," I said. "I'd best get out there. I'll be back next week to check the fences."

"That'll be just fine, Eric," Mr. Hazard said.

I rode away knowing Mama was partly right about the charity. Mr. Hazard didn't really need me to

35

check the fences. But the Hazards' two boys were grown, and they always had food left over. Having me mend the fence was Mr. Hazard's way of keeping me from feeling in debt.

At the creek Willie and Tom were already splashing around in the water. I left my horse with theirs, shed my sweaty clothes and dived into the water beside them. When Papa was alive, we three used to spend half the summer swimming in that creek. Now there were always too many chores to be done. We still got down to the creek from time to time, though.

Tom and I would never have played around much at the creek by ourselves, but Willie was half fish, and he was always popping up from underwater, splashing us or screaming and getting in the way. I thought several times we'd end up drowning poor little Willie.

It was only late June, but we were already about as bronze as Mama's George Washington bookends. I loved the way I looked in summer, and I noticed how alike Tom was getting to be to me. He always had been a little thinner. I'd never been tall for my age, and I had kind of big shoulders for a boy of twelve. Tom was more like a pole, skinny and with a long neck. Willie was even skinnier. You could count Willie's ribs when he was bare.

After a couple of hours in the creek we got back into our clothes and headed home. Willie griped about going back so early, but didn't say anything else after Tom threatened to roll him around in the horses' stalls when we got back.

I left Willie and Tom in the barn tending the horses and walked into the house. I wiped the sweat from my forehead and dumped a dipper of water over my head. Then I swallowed a cupful of water and set down the sack of potatoes and carrots.

"Mama?" I called to her. "You all right?"

"Just fine, son," she said.

I walked into her room and sat down in my usual place on the side of her bed.

"I brought some potatoes from Mr. Hazard's place," I told her. "I thought maybe we could fry a chicken tonight. Tomorrow we'll have fresh beef. Things're looking better."

"Better," she said, smiling at me. "Eric, you're really something."

"You knew that all along, Mama," I said, smiling back at her. "But you're not sure just what, are you?"

She sat up and grabbed my arm. Then she pulled me to her and hugged me tightly against her warm shoulder.

"It shouldn't be so hard on you," she said.

"It is, though," I told her. "Not much we can do about that."

"Yes, there is," Mama said. "I've been doing a lot of thinking about it. It just isn't right for you boys to be working so hard here. And what will you do when school starts?"

"We'll have to tend to our chores early," I said. "I'll stay home when I have to."

"Your father would turn over in his grave, Eric. No, that won't do, not at all."

"Then what're we going to do?" I asked. "We sure can't go into town and live."

"No," she said. "We can't do that. I've written a wire to your Uncle Sam. You remember how I've talked about the big ranch he has down in Texas? He's got a son just a little older than you. A man always needs boys on a ranch."

"I'm not going away," I said. "We have a ranch right here."

"A ranch?" she said, laughing. "You call this a

ranch? All we have here is an open prairie fenced in for cows. There's only the creek for water, and it doesn't rain half the summer. Eric, when we had the store, there was a future here for you boys. Now there's nothing."

"We'll get the store back, Mama," I said. "Dunstan won't stay forever."

"Don't you ever mention that name in my house again!" Mama shouted, her face red as an apple.

"Yes, ma'am," I said. "Look, Mama, men like that don't stay. They ride through a town and steal everything they can. Then they ride on. When they're gone, we'll get the store back."

"And how many of us will be buried out there on that hill with your father and brother and sister? How many of you boys will be left? Eric, it's for you most of all."

"Mama, you don't understand," I said. "Papa told me about it one time. He said that hill out there's our collection box. It's what we've paid to hold this land."

"The price was too high," Mama said.

"Too high to cut and run," I told her. "I watched Papa die. I saw him fight to keep what's ours. I can't just run away 'cause it's tough."

"Eric, I've made up my mind about this," she said.

"And I've made up mine," I told her. "If you want Tom and Willie to go, if you want to go yourself, then go. But I won't ever leave this place. You said a man has to belong to something. I do. I belong right here, to this land."

"No piece of land is worth dying for," Mama said.

"Then what is worth dying for?" I asked. "When do you ever stop running? You're the one with all the stories about the Delamers. You're the one who told me about your grandfather coming from France,

38

going to Texas, dying in the war against the Mexicans. What do you expect me to do?"

"Mind your mother," she said sternly.

"I will, Mama. I'll send the wire. But I won't go. I won't stay little forever. When I'm big enough, I'll get them all. They won't laugh then."

"Oh, Eric," she said, crying. "We should have gone away after your father died."

"After he died?" I said, raising my eyebrows. "Papa didn't die. He was murdered. It wasn't like with Michael. It wasn't the chill of winter that took him away. It was a bullet!"

"You've got to put all that behind you, son," she said.

"Never," I told her. "Not until they're all lying in their graves."

Then I took the message she'd written and started for town.

V

Town was only a mile away, and I didn't like to take my horse. Sometimes Dunstan's men saw a horse they liked and just took it. The kind of men they were, it didn't bother them that they might take a man's only horse. Maybe a whole farm's crops might not get put in the ground on account of it. Anyway, that's why I always walked into town.

When I passed the little Mexican cantina on the outskirts of Whitlow, I slid into the shadows, avoiding everyone. It was hot outside, and most people kept in the shade of porches during the afternoon.

When I got to the telegraph office, I walked inside and handed Mama's note to Mr. Lee, the operator.

"This is all the way to Texas, Eric?" he asked.

"Yes, sir," I told him. "It's for my uncle."

"You know what it says, boy? You all really leaving?"

"Not me, Mr. Lee," I said. "I think maybe Tom and Willie might be going out there."

"I think maybe you should go, too, Eric," he said. "It might do you a world of good to get away from this town for a while. You can always come back, son."

"Yes, sir," I said.

"Won't be the same without Sheidlers in this town, though. You all been here from the beginning. I remember when your pa and you put the feed store up. Before that . . ."

"Yes, sir," I said. "I remember, too. Is a dollar enough for the wire?"

"A quarter to spare," he said, taking the money and giving me the change. "If there's an answer, I'll drop it by on my way home."

"That's all right, sir," I told him. "I'll check for it when I come to town the next time."

"There's no charge, Eric. I go right by your house every night. It'd be my privilege to do this favor for your ma."

"Well, I guess it'd be all right then," I said. "Thank you, sir."

"You look out for yourself, Eric," he said as I left.

I walked quietly back along the line of shops homeward. People smiled and nodded or said hello, but I had no eyes for their smiles, no ears for their words. I stumbled along, bouncing off wooden posts and benches, barely managing to keep from falling into a watering trough.

As I passed the saloon, I took a quick peek out of my left eye. None of Dunstan's men were around, so I ran by. As I passed the door, Mitch Ryan came charging out, banging into me and knocking me to the ground.

"Watch where you're going, stupid clumsy boy!" Ryan yelled.

A couple of men laughed from the saloon, and Ryan took me by the arm.

"Let go of me," I said, twisting to escape his grasp.

"Well, I got myself a real tiger, boys!" he yelled to the men in the saloon. "Come take a look."

41

Three of them walked out and gathered around me.

"I'll bet a boy like this bounces. Here, Jack," Ryan said, pushing me at a young man about five feet away.

I stumbled to one knee, but the man named Jack picked me up and pushed me back. The other two men gathered around, and soon the four of them were tossing me around like a child's rag doll.

"Leave me alone," I told them. "You'll pay for this."

"Just having a bit of fun," Ryan said, kicking me in the ribs so that I lost my breath. "You're the Sheidler kid, ain't you?"

I bit my lip and stared hard at him.

"You remember me," I said.

"Here, Mitch," one of them said, tossing me back to Ryan. I hit hard against his knee and fell to the ground, stunned.

"Now you've gone and hurt him," one of them said. "Look, the poor little boy's gone and hurt his head."

As Ryan turned away laughing, I reached for his pistol. In a flash I had the gun and pointed it at him.

"Now laugh, Ryan," I said, waving the gun at him. "Now you laugh like Hunt did when he shot my father! Now laugh while your guts are lying on the street!"

"What's this?" Ryan asked, pretending to be scared. "Now you wouldn't want to go and shoot old Mitch, now would you? We've got laws in Colorado, you know. We'd have to string you up. That'd be a shame, stringing up such a fine, good-looking boy like you."

"I wouldn't be laughing at a man holding a gun on me, stranger," spoke a voice I hadn't heard before.

"Might just go off. Now why don't you boys just back off a bit?"

By this time a crowd had gathered, and the people murmured their agreement.

"This is our business, stranger," Ryan said. "You'd be best to stay out of it."

"Maybe I should," the stranger said. "You'd look right nice with an extra belly button."

Ryan frowned. It wasn't a joke anymore.

"Give me my gun, Sheidler," Ryan said. "I swear if you don't, I'll peel you like an apple."

"You wouldn't want to give a boy a toy like that," the stranger said, pointing at Ryan. "He might hurt himself. Some other person might take it away from him."

I backed away from Ryan. The others gave me room, and I felt my back touch something hard as rock.

"Why don't you give me that pistol?" the stranger said. "You don't really want to shoot anybody, do you?"

I felt a hand on my shoulder, and I turned to look up into the eyes of a man I'd never seen before.

"Give me the gun, son," the man said to me.

I handed it to him.

"I'll take that," Ryan said, reaching for the pistol.

"When you grow up," the stranger said, tossing the gun into the watering trough. "Cool off a bit."

"I'll remember you, stranger," Ryan said as the man led me away. "You'll be hearing from me."

"Seems likely," the stranger said. "Seems like you talk better and more than most."

Then the man led me off down the street and sat down with me on a bench in front of the stage office.

"You've got a few scratches," he said. "Best get home and let your ma tend to them."

43

"I can tend to myself," I told him.

"I see that," he said. "How old are you?"

"Nearly thirteen," I said, trying to sit up taller.

"Twelve then," he said, shaking his head. "Little young to be fighting gunmen."

"They started it," I said.

"Is it always like this here?" he asked. "Grown men stand around and let a couple of two bit toughs like that kick a kid around?"

"They're gunmen. They've shot people. The men in this town aren't good with guns. They'd just get themselves killed."

"A man who lets a boy get kicked around and does nothing can't even be called a man," the stranger said. "You live here?"

"Just outside of town," I said.

"Better come in with your pa next time around," he said, helping me to my feet.

"My father's dead," I said, looking at the ground. "A man named Hunt shot him. Papa never had a chance."

"Don't you have any law here?" the man asked.

"We had a sheriff, a good one," I said. "Sheriff Campbell. The first day those men rode into town they killed him right on the street. Since then they just do what they want."

"You alone with your ma?" the man asked.

"No, sir," I said. "I've got two brothers, both younger. We make out all right."

"Do you now? You haven't maybe tended a horse or two in your time, have you?"

"Night and day, sir. I've even made poultices for sore feet. Soon as I get big enough I'll be able to shoe a horse, too. Mr. Roderick down at the livery promised to teach me."

"Well, boy, you see that black stallion there?" he

44

asked, pointing to a tall black horse caked with mud and dust. "He's mine. There's four bits in it if you'll stable and wash him. Rub him down real good. He's been rode hard. Give him some oats. You know where the stable is?"

"Yes, sir," I said. "I'll brush him till he shines. He'll be the proudest stallion in the territory of Colorado."

"You meet me in the saloon when you finish, son," he said. "That's where I'll be."

"Yes, sir," I said as he walked away.

As he left, I marveled at the way he was put together. Every part of him seemed like a piece of some new machine. There wasn't an inch of fat on him, and every muscle seemed taut, coiled like a rattlesnake ready to strike.

He'd once been a somebody, that was clear. He had a way of walking, a way of holding his head that forced you to look up at him. He wasn't a tall man, but he seemed tall.

He'd come a long way. There was a smell of horses and campfires about him. His beard was scraggly, and his boots were covered with mud and muck.

I'd never seen a man dressed like he was. He wore a buckskin jacket and trousers. His shirt was once white cotton, but it was stained and dirty now. Oddest of all, he wore the hat of a Confederate cavalry officer on his head.

I thought for a minute it was just my imagination, but when I saw the C. S. A. across the front of the hat, I was sure.

As he left, the thing I remembered was his eyes. They were blue, like my own, but they weren't like the eyes of any living man I'd ever seen. They were like Papa's after he died. They were cold, unfeeling, dead. There was a warmth to the man's touch, but his eyes

45

were as cold as death itself.

It was strange. He was obviously a man of pride, but his clothes were in rags. His jacket had a bad tear in one sleeve, and his shirt was so worn you could see through it in parts.

He carried around his waist a belt with the biggest gun I'd ever seen. The barrel was a good two inches longer than Papa's. He also carried a knife in a scabbard on his boot.

The man looked to be about forty. His walk was that of a younger man, and I figured maybe he'd had a rough time of it. Maybe his father had died when he was little, too. Maybe he'd had to grow up fast.

As I thought about it, his horse whinnied, and I got to my feet. Then I took the reins of the horse and led it down the street to the stable.

When I walked inside the stable, Mr. Roderick glanced up from his forge and smiled.

"What's that you got there, Eric?" he asked. "Looks like a lot of horse for so small a boy."

"A stranger turned him over to me, Mr. Roderick," I said. "He said to wash him, rub him down and feed him."

"I don't suppose he gave you anything to pay for all that with, did he?" the man asked.

"No, sir," I said. "He went into the saloon. He looked like he'd been riding quite a bit."

"Hard, too," Mr. Roderick said, looking at the horse. "Did you ever see a finer animal in your life, boy?"

"No, sir," I said. "He rode it like a general, too. He looked like he'd seen some rough times lately, but there's something about him."

"Another gunman," Mr. Roderick said, frowning. "They'll likely take my place next. This whole town will be drying up. But when people like your pa gets shot down in the street by the likes of Dunstan's men, the decent people better start packing their bags."

"Yes, sir," I said, leading the horse to a stall and loosening the cinch.

"Well, I'll be," Mr. Roderick said as I heaved the saddle onto the side of the stall. "This here's a cavalry saddle. Haven't seen one around here in quite a spell."

"A cavalry saddle?" I asked, looking at it. "It looks like any other saddle."

"No, son," the man said, pointing to it with his dirty fingers. "See how the back of the saddle's cut away. There's only a little bit of leather between you and the horse. Takes a tough man to use this kind of saddle. An ordinary kind of a man would have his rump split wide open after a few miles. The man that rides this horse is a man used to riding."

"You should have seen him, sir. He's a strange man."

"Strange? How do you mean?"

"His eyes, sir. They sort of look right through you. He isn't the kind of man you'd want to tangle with. He looks like he could kill you real easy."

"One of Dunstan's new hands," Mr. Roderick said.

"I don't think so," I said. "He's different. He didn't say anything about Dunstan, didn't ask where to find him or anything like that. Dunstan's men usually come on the train. I never saw one of Dunstan's men on a horse like this. And he carried a pistol with a long barrel, longer than even that man of Dunstan's named Kincaid."

"You think he's a lawman?" Mr. Roderick asked.

"No, sir," I said. "He doesn't have the eye of a lawman. He just looked right through Ryan when Ryan threatened me. I'd say he was a wandering kind of man, a drifter."

"Likely," Mr. Roderick said.

Mr. Roderick went back to the forge, and I took the horse over to the trough and started splashing water over him. The dust washed away, and the horse seemed even grander than before. His dark black coat began to shine as I brushed it, and the horse dipped his head across my shoulder.

"Good boy," I said, stroking the horse's nose. "Would you look at this horse, Mr. Roderick?"

"Well, I'll be, Eric," he said. "Who'd you say brought in this stallion? He's a prize."

"He didn't say what his name was," I said. "He's not a big man, maybe not even six feet tall. But what there is of him's put together, sir."

"How old is he?"

"Oh, forty or so. He looks older than Papa did. He might not be that old. I don't know. There's something confusing about him."

"Forty's too old for a top gun hand," Mr. Roderick said. "Dunstan doesn't need anymore errand boys. You might be right. He may not be with Dunstan."

"Besides," I said, laughing. "He told me he'd pay me for tending his horse. Dunstan would've said do it or else."

"What else did you notice about him?" he asked.

"He was in the Confederate cavalry," I said. "He had an officer's hat on. It was pretty dusty, but it still had the C. S. A. and the crossed swords on the front."

"What else did he wear?"

"Pretty ragged clothes," I said. "His coat had a tear in the sleeve. He wore some kind of buckskin boots. Indian kind of boots. And he had a knife in a scabbard on his leg."

"Doesn't mean anything at all. Sounds like a hundred men who come riding through here every day."

"I know," I said.

"But the horse and the saddle, now that's something. My guess'd be a cavalryman. Strange he'd keep that rebel hat. The war's been over ten years. I wonder what he's been doing all this time. You suppose he's one of them rebels that never surrendered?"

"I don't think so, Mr. Roderick. He looks to me like he's done a lot of surrendering. He's pretty worn out, if you ask me. If it hadn't been for his horse and those eyes of his, I'd call him a saddle bum."

"You think he's got money for the horse's feed?" Mr. Roderick asked.

"I would if I rode a horse like this one," I said. "He's a well fed horse. I'd say he has the money. But if Dunstan gets a look at the horse, I imagine the stranger won't have a horse anymore."

"Put him in the end stall," Mr. Roderick said. "Turn his backside to the door. And give him half a sack of oats."

"Yes, sir," I said.

When the horse had eaten his fill, I filled his water bucket and stepped back.

"I'll be around later, Mr. Roderick. You'll keep an eye on the horse?" I asked him.

"I won't fight Dunstan over it," he said.

"If anybody asks after it, let me know. All right?"

"Sure, Eric," the man said, laughing loudly. "Then you can go over and scare the man away."

"Then I can tell the stranger," I said. "Maybe he'll get rid of Dunstan for us."

"And maybe that Yankee president will send a regiment of cavalry. Maybe the governor in Denver will send us a marshal. Maybe they'll all die in their sleep."

I walked away from the stable. We didn't need a

marshal or a regiment of cavalry. If the whole town had stood up when my father tried to get them to stand together, Dunstan would be gone already. But instead the feed store had been stolen away from us, and I had a tombstone for a father.

VI

It took me only a few minutes to get to the saloon. My mother didn't like me hanging around there, but this was business. The stranger owed me half a dollar for taking care of his horse, and there was no other way of collecting. At least that was what I'd tell Mama if she heard I was there.

The truth of the matter was that I wanted to see what was going to happen. If the stranger was one of Dunstan's men, this was a sure-fire way of finding out. If he wasn't, it would be interesting to find out how Dunstan's men treated him.

The stranger sat at the bar. He slowly sipped a mug of beer. There was nothing very promising about what was happening. Through the swinging doors I could see several men sitting around playing cards. About half of them were Dunstan's men, but none of the top guns were there.

"What you looking at?" asked someone behind me.

"Who, me?" I asked, trying to shrink.

"Yeah, you!" said Tripp Hunt, ginning so that his moustache curled up around the corners of his mouth.

"Nothing, Mr. Hunt, I said, backing away.

"You're the Sheidler kid, aren't you?" he asked, smiling. "Tough luck about your pa. You know some people don't know how to get out of the way."

"I guess so," I said, biting down on my lip.

"Like your attitude, boy," he said. "I never shot no little boy before. You keep your mind nice and clear, son. I'd surely hate for you to be lying out there in the churchyard with your pa. With nobody around to take care of your ma, she might find herself with some unwelcome company."

"Got anybody in mind?" I asked sarcastically.

"Watch the mouth, boy," Hunt said, walking through the doors and on into the saloon.

I watched Hunt with hatred. Everybody in town knew he was the one who shot my father. He bragged about it even. I wanted to stand up to him, but Hunt was just mean enough to shoot a kid right on the street. Sometimes fear has a way of keeping you alive.

Once Hunt walked inside the saloon, everything changed. He walked right up to the bar and bumped into the stranger.

"Watch where you're sitting," Hunt said, laughing. "You'd think some people would know better than to be getting in the way of a real man. Right, old man?"

The stranger moved away a few feet and glared at Hunt.

"You hear me, old man?" Hunt said, setting down the glass handed him by the bartender.

"Hey, Tripp," Ryan said, standing up at one of the card tables, "this dude was sticking his nose in our fun a little while back. We were pushing the Sheidler kid around some, and he took offense. Seems kind of taken with Sheidlers."

"That so?" Hunt asked the stranger. "Maybe you

come to town to work for old lady Sheidler?"

The stranger just ignored Hunt and sipped the beer mug.

"Hey, I'm talking to you!" Hunt shouted.

"Now, Tripp, you know the management don't take to no fighting inside," the bartender said. "Why don't you and the gentleman take your disagreement on outside?"

"How about it? You want to settle this outside?" Hunt asked the stranger.

The newcomer still ignored him, and Hunt grew angry.

"You hear me?" Hunt asked. "You deaf or something?"

Hunt grabbed the stranger's shoulder and started to pull him away from the bar, but the stranger pushed the gunman away and stood up.

"You talking to me?" the stranger asked in a calm voice, casting his cold eyes across Hunt's face.

"You know I was talking to you. You want to go outside and settle this?" Hunt asked.

The stranger cracked a slight smile. Hunt's face was red as a strawberry, and already the gunman's hand was slapping against his holster.

"Settle what?" the stranger finally asked.

"Well, I see what you mean," Hunt said. "What you really want to do is apologize, right? You want to beg my pardon for not moving faster."

Hunt exchanged a smile with the men at the card tables.

"Apologize for what?" the stranger asked without changing expression.

"Well, what we have here is a needed lesson in manners," Hunt said.

"I agree," the stranger said. "But I'm a little busy just now. See me tomorrow, boy, and I'll give it to

53

you."

I began to smile. Here was a man you could look up to. Here was a man that wasn't going to take anything from anybody.

"Well, I guess you don't know much about this town," Hunt said. "This is my town, mister. I run it because I can shoot the buttons off your underwear. In this town people speak lightly when I'm around."

"Where I come from," the stranger said, "a man doesn't run a town with his mouth. And he knows better than to press a man he doesn't know about. I've stood and watched many a man put in the ground who talked when he should have thought."

The men at the card tables chuckled, and Hunt's face grew red again.

"You know I didn't notice it before, but you've got one of them rebel hats on, don't you?" Hunt said. "Pig hats we call them. 'Course a pig don't really need a hat. You don't really need it now, do you?"

Hunt walked toward the man and reached out to take the hat. The stranger stepped back and took Hunt's hand in his own. Then with a single quick movement, the stranger sent Hunt sprawling on the floor.

"You'll pay for that!" Hunt shouted.

"Glad to," the stranger said, calm as ever. "Here's a quarter."

"You rebs forget the lesson we taught you in the war," Hunt said, backing toward the door. "I heard my brother talk about how we burned out the whole of the Shenandoah Valley. 'Course a lot of you pigs forgot. Some of us don't. Some can't. My brother died in the valley, shot down by a bunch of reb cavalry. I'll bet you was leading them. I'm not one of them that forgets easy. I remember. You hear what I'm saying? My brother was killed by stinkin' rebs

54

ike you. Stinkin' pigs that don't even know how to
ake a bath. Maybe we ought to show you how to
ake a bath. What do you say, boys?"

The men at the table laughed, but a glance from
he stranger hushed them.

"Well, reb," Hunt said, "I'll give you a choice. You
ake your stinkin' hide and get out of here so we
lecent folks can enjoy ourselves, or . . ."

"Or what?" the stranger asked.

"Or maybe we'll be having to carry you out," Hunt
;aid.

"I tell you, big mouth, I'd leave, but I've been
·idin' since early morning. I'm tired. My horse is
ired. He's getting himself a drink down at the livery,
and I'm getting myself a drink here. I'm thirsty, you
;ee. When I'm thirsty, I drink. Besides, if your
orother was like you, the Confederate army did the
whole world a lot of good. Now be a good boy and
·un along. Play your game with somebody who's got
the time."

There was a snicker from the card table, and Hunt
stepped away from the door. He spread his hands
back, and the stranger turned to face him. The whole
saloon was filled with deathlike silence. Everyone
waited for one of the men to make a move.

Hunt was filled with anger. His mouth was open
slightly, and he twitched. His hands were sweaty and
a little shaky. It was the first time I ever saw him
hesitate.

The stranger was cool as ice. He just stared at
Hunt, his lips moist. The stranger's eyes blazed with
a fire that came all of a sudden, and he held his hand
still at his side. This was a picture of pure concentration. Not a movement, not even a blink came from
the stranger.

The others scattered. The bartender hit the floor,

and the other men moved to the back of the saloon. [leaned against the door, ready to duck out of the way the instant the shooting started.

"Anytime you feel like it, stranger," Hunt said.

The stranger said nothing.

Finally Hunt reached for his pistol. A single shot rang through the room, and Hunt's face went white. Then Hunt toppled through the swinging doors, rolling over beside my feet.

One of the dance girls screamed, and three or four men raced to Hunt's side. I looked down on the body of my father's murderer. There was a single circle of red just above his right eye. Hunt was dead.

In the second before Hunt's friends got there, I spit on the man's face. Then I stepped back from him as I realized what I'd seen.

"What happened?" asked some of the townspeople, running down the street. "Who got shot?"

"Tripp Hunt," I said, trying to keep my stomach down.

"Hunt?" asked Mr. Warren, who had owned the mercantile. "Who did it? Did he fall out with Dunstan?"

"It was a stranger," I said. "I never saw him before. He's cool, Mr. Warren. Hunt pressed him, and now Hunt's dead. He's not a man to be tangled with. He's just what this town needs."

"Well, I can't fault him for gunning down a man like Hunt, but gunplay in Whitlow isn't exactly what I'd like to see. Besides, now he'll end up getting killed. Dunstan won't let anyone get away with killing one of his men," Mr. Warren said.

"I don't suppose he will," I said, frowning.

Some men carried Hunt down the street to the undertaker's, and the crowd moved apart as the stranger walked into the street. I stared at the man.

He hadn't changed the expression on his face the slightest bit.

"He went back and finished his beer," someone whispered. "He's a cold-blooded killer!"

I watched the man stop when he got to the center of the street. He turned and looked through the crowd. His cold eyes searched for something. Then they fixed themselves on me.

"Hey boy!" the man called to me. "You were supposed to wait for me by the door."

"Yes, sir," I said, running to him. "I . . . I was scared. The shooting started, and then all the people ran out and . . ."

"How old did you say you were, son?" he asked, laughing.

"Twelve," I told him. "A little older than that."

"You got a name?"

"Sure," I said. "Eric Sheidler. It's a good name."

"Can't find any fault with it," he said. "Well, Eric Sheidler, let's go see my horse."

"I did a real fine job, sir," I said. "I washed him and brushed him. I got Mr. Roderick to give him half a bag of oats. He was worried about getting paid, but I told him you were good for it."

"I have a trustworthy face, huh?" he asked.

"Yes, sir," I said. "I figure a man who has a horse like that pays his feed bills."

"You've got a good head, boy. Let's see how you are with horses."

We walked inside the stable together. Mr. Roderick glanced up at the man and shuddered.

"Who put my horse in the stall like that?" the stranger asked. "You've stuck his nose in the wall."

"It was my idea," I said. "The men who run this town steal horses sometimes. I figured they might not notice him if his backside was to the door."

57

"You don't think he's got a pretty backside, huh?" the man asked, cracking a smile. "Turn him around. Nobody's going to steal him as long as I'm alive. After I'm dead, it really doesn't much matter."

"Yes, sir," I said, walking into the stall and turning the horse around.

"You did a fine job of it, son," the man said. "A fine job. You're a man to be taken at his word."

"Thank you, sir," I said, catching in my hands the two quarters he tossed me.

"What do I owe you to stable my horse, mister?" the stranger asked Mr. Roderick.

"My customers mostly pay as they leave, sir," Mr. Roderick said.

"I have a habit of leaving at odd times," the man said. "How much for a week with feed and water and a turn around the barn three times a day?"

"You'll have to do your own exercising," Mr. Roderick said. "Feed and water's a dollar a day. Twenty dollars a month."

"Seems a little high," the stranger said.

"Well, I make nothing off half my customers," Mr. Roderick explained. "The rest have to pay a little more."

"See what you mean," the man said. "Here's a ten dollar gold piece. If I leave before the time's out, give the balance to the boy."

"Yes, sir," Mr. Roderick said.

"That's mighty kind, sir," I said. "That's a lot of money, though."

"You'll earn it," he told me. "I want you to come down to the stable and turn my horse around the barn three times a day. If his feet look to need it, you'll take him on a short ride early in the morning so nobody'll see it."

"Yes, sir," I said. "Sir, are you not wanting to be

58

seen by somebody? You can trust me. I wouldn't be telling anyone. There isn't any sheriff. Nearest law's in Pueblo, and he's got no interest stirring up trouble for himself here."

"I'm not wanted anywhere," the stranger said. "You suppose you could show me the hotel? I'm in bad need of a meal and a bath."

"Sure," I said, leading the way.

VII

As I led the way to the hotel, I noticed the other townspeople staring at us. Some seemed glad to have a man in town to stand up to Dunstan. Others seemed fearful. Most looked at us with eyes filled with suspicion.

At the hotel I led the way to the front desk.

"Hello, Eric," said Mr. Garner, the manager. "How's your mother holding up?"

"Okay," I said, looking away from him. "Mr. Garner, this man needs a room and a bath."

"Your name, sir?" Mr. Garner asked.

"They call me Fletcher, Jack Fletcher," the man said. "It's as good a name as any."

"Wait just a minute," Mr. Garner said, pulling the register away from the man. "You're the one everybody's talking about. Why I bet your gun's still hot. I don't house killers in my hotel, no, sir."

"But Mr. Garner," I said, "it was Tripp Hunt. He's a man that needed killing."

"That's even worse," Mr. Garner said. "It'd only bring trouble. I don't want my hotel all shot up."

"How about a meal then?" asked the man called Fletcher. "Got anything against feeding a man?"

"Not unless he's a killer," Mr. Garner said. "Then he'd best find eating elsewhere."

"Mr. Garner, it's the same as if I killed Hunt," I said. "You'd put me up, wouldn't you?"

"Eric, your father was like a brother to me, but I wouldn't rent even you a room if you killed one of Dunstan's men," Mr. Garner said. "You know they'll come after him."

"Come after me?" the stranger asked. "Who?"

"Dunstan," I said. "But who cares about him? You killed Hunt. He was mean and fast, real fast. You got him before he could even get off a shot."

"That's the safest way," the man said. "This man Dunstan, is he a big man? Wears a black hat with a nick in the front? Carries twin .44's?"

"That's him," I said. "He'll probably send some men to get you. You'll have to watch out. He's had men shot in the back."

"I'll keep an eye open. Seems likely he'll send somebody," Fletcher said, waving me out of the hotel.

"You don't even seem scared," I said as we walked out onto the street. "Hunt killed five men in this town. You didn't even blink."

"A man can be dead in the blink of an eye," he told me. "How come you know so much about this Hunt?"

"He killed my father," I said, trying to keep my voice calm. "Dunstan wanted our store. Papa wouldn't give it up, so Dunstan sent Hunt. Hunt just walked in, looked my father over and shot him down."

"Why'd Dunstan want your store?"

"It was the best feed store east of Pueblo," I said. "Papa kept the prices down, treated folks right. Farmers have to buy feed for their animals, seed for

61

their crops. Now they have to buy from Dunstan."

"You don't care too much for Dunstan, huh?" he asked.

"If he'd killed your father, would you?" I asked. "He's mean, and he doesn't care who gets hurt. He'd as soon shoot me as not. When I get bigger, I'll kill him."

"You've got a lot of growing to do before that, boy," the man told me.

"Call me Eric," I said. Everybody does. I'm a man now that Papa's dead. It's not right to call a man 'boy.' "

"All right, son, where do I find something to eat?" he asked.

"Do you like tamales?" I asked. "There's a place on the edge of town that serves 'em hot and crispy. Papa used to take me there sometimes."

"Seems worth a try then," Fletcher said.

Moments later we were sitting at a table in the cantina, waiting for Maria Enuncia to bring Fletcher his dinner. That was when the man looked me in the eye and frowned.

"Son, tell me the whole works," he said. "Tell me everything you know about Dunstan and his men. Describe them. I want names, the hardware they carry, any habits they have. You give me all of it now."

"Yes, sir," I said. "There are about ten or so of them that can shoot. Some of 'em just do Dunstan's leg work. First came Dunstan himself. He shot Sheriff Campbell down right in the street. Then the others came, and Dunstan started taking over. He's got a saloon, the bank, the feed store and the mercantile. He watches the telegraph key. The train and the stage still stop, but he's shut off the mail."

"And the people just stood and watched?"

"They're scared. Papa and some of the others stood up to Dunstan. One by one they got themselves shot."

"How many guns has Dunstan got?"

"Nine now that Hunt's dead."

"Who?"

"Well," I said, scratching my head, "first there's Jacobs. Then there's Ryan and Hardesty and . . ."

"Just the ones faster than Hunt," he said.

"That makes it a lot easier," I said. "There're just two. I've never seen Dunstan shoot, though. I wasn't around when he shot the sheriff."

"Tell me about them."

"The first is a little man. He chews tobacco, and you can't hear him too good. He carried a gun with a long barrel, like yours. The stock's smaller, though. His name starts with a K."

"That'd be Kincaid," Fletcher said, frowning. "The other one would be tall. He walks with a limp and carries a Winchester rifle most of the time. He uses a Smith and Wesson to do his killing. That's Corby Johnson."

"You know 'em?" I asked.

"Of them," he said. "Johnson's the faster. He's a dead shot, a real dangerous man."

"Faster than you?" I asked.

"Don't plan to find out," he said.

"Dunstan always sends his men to kill," I said. "It'll be one or the other of them."

"Doesn't matter," he said. "I won't be here. Only a fool plays with a man holding all the aces."

"You mean you'd just leave, walk out on us?"

"I don't owe this town a thing," he said. "They won't even put me up in the hotel. Now just how am I supposed to feel? I'll sleep in no barn like a horse. As soon as I pick up something at the freight depot,

63

I'll be on my way."

"What?"

"On my way, Eric. Look, son, you're the only one in this town I've met so far with half a backbone. If you live long enough, you'll grow into a fair man. Get someone to ride to Denver and tell the governor. Maybe some troops'll come. I'm no marshal. Believe me, I'm sure not that!"

"You're an outlaw," I said with a sigh. "I should have known."

"I never done a single thing against the law," he said angrily. "I believe in laws, son, but there's laws and laws. Sometimes a man makes his own, like Dunstan. There's one real law out here. The strong make the rules, and the weak die."

"And what about people like me?" I asked, shaking. "Am I supposed to die?"

"You?" he said, laughing. "You were born a scrapper. You'll never die in bed, son. You'll be hitting 'em when they put the sheet over your head."

"We could lick 'em, you and me. I know the town, every place there is to hide. We could get 'em one by one."

"Son, you don't expect me to kill ten men, do you? Two of them are fast guns, not counting Dunstan. He killed fifty men down on the Cimarron, you know."

"Did you know him back then?" I asked.

"Seen him shoot. He can stitch a man neat as my mama could stitch a pair of trousers."

"I guess there's nothing more to say," I said. "I thought maybe you were different from the other men in town."

"Nobody takes a shine to getting shot. Nobody."

"I know," I said. "I'm scared, too."

Maria brought Fletcher a plate of tamales and set a bowl of chili in front of me.

"You like to eat?" she asked, handing me a spoon.

"I have to save my money, Maria," I told her.

"I not ask for money from you, little one," she said. "I feed you for joy of seeing you smile. Eat. Is good chili."

I never needed much encouragement to eat, so I took the spoon and began eating the chili.

"This is very fine tamales, senorita," Fletcher said. "How much do I owe you?"

"Nothing," Maria said, smiling. "There is never charge for man who kill Tripp Hunt. He was very fast with a gun. He also was very fast at taking away what others put in their pockets. He take from us our money and our pride. Such a man is better dead. People have need of their pride."

"Yes," Fletcher said, his eyes cold. "Gracias."

"Si, senor," Maria said, smiling. "Go with God, senor."

"Good-bye," I said to Maria as we left.

"Take care, little Eric," she said. "This one is strange."

As we walked to the stables, her words haunted me. I pointed the way inside the place, but Fletcher turned away.

"Don't you want your horse?" I asked. "I know Mr. Roderick will give you back your money. He's an honest man."

"Don't want it back," he said. "What's left over is yours."

"I won't take money from a stranger," I said. "That's charity. Besides, it'd just be something else for Dunstan to steal."

"It's a gift," he said. "I have no need of it."

"I never asked you for anything," I said. "The undertaker's place is this way," I added, leading the way. "Why go there, though?"

"I want to find out when they're going to bury Hunt," he said as we walked.

"Eleven o'clock," I said. "They never wait around in the summer. As soon as they can get a man into a coffin, they get the grave dug."

"Do they have a service?" he asked.

"Yes," I said. "Reverend Manchester reads over everybody, even the likes of Hunt. He says special words over some people. He spoke special words for Papa. No matter who it is, though, they always have the funeral at eleven."

"Then we'd best head for the churchyard," he said. "We have to pay our respects."

"Not me," I said, stopping. "I won't go to the funeral of the man who killed my father."

"Don't you think God knows what he did? Don't you think God knows everything we do each day? Let Him do the judging, Eric. You got to forgive. The man's going to burn for all eternity. Don't that seem enough to you?"

"No," I said, my eyes full of hatred. "Every time I see Papa's grave I'll remember how Hunt shot him down."

"You've got a hardness inside you for someone who isn't very big, Eric. You ought to let it heal."

"How?" I asked. "You're riding away from here. I have to watch them rob this town until there's nothing left. I have to wait until I'm big enough to shoot a gun. Then I'll kill them, every single one of them!"

"Seems a sad future to plan for yourself," Fletcher said.

"It could be better," I said. "You could stay, at least long enough to teach me to shoot. Then I'd be fast enough to take care of them myself."

"No twelve-year-old's ever going to outdraw a man, especially a man who's killed before. Kids always

66

hesitate. Just a second. Just long enough to get themselves killed."

"I guess you've killed a lot of men, huh?"

"Too many," he said. "I watched thousands die in the war, but this killing face to face is different. You see their eyes, hear their breath, smell their bodies as they wait to die."

"It didn't seem to bother you in the saloon," I said. "They say you even finished your beer. I nearly threw up."

"There comes a time when everything is cold, son," he told me. "There's nothing to the killing anymore. It's just like plowing a field or riding a horse. It's been practiced till all the rough edges are gone."

"You mean you don't even think about the men?" I asked.

"Thinking gets you killed," he said. "When I shoot a man, it's just done. That's all there is to it. I go to the funeral and pray he'll find salvation. Listen, son, I never in all my life went looking for trouble. Trouble always finds me. When a man comes looking for me, he'd better know he's going to die. That's the only way the kids know to stay away. Dying's a pretty final type of a thing."

"Yes, sir," I said. "I know it is."

VIII

Reverend Manchester had a difficult time reading over Tripp Hunt. There really wasn't much that could be said about Hunt. He was a cruel, heartless kind of man. The reverend said all sinners can be redeemed, but I remembered the laughing face of the man who had stood over my dead father.

Papa once told me you could tell a lot about a man's life by the people who came to his funeral. Mr. Fletcher and I stood to one side. Reverend Manchester stood beside the coffin. Only a weeping girl who'd worked in the saloon stood on the other side of the simple pine box.

When the minister finished praying for Hunt's soul, he sprinkled some dirt over the coffin as it was lowered into the grave. Mr. Fletcher did the same. I just walked away.

"Son," Reverend Manchester said, pulling me to him. "Eric, you show a forgiving heart by coming here this day."

"It wasn't my idea," I told him. "Mr. Fletcher said to come. I haven't forgiven anyone. I'm only glad Papa isn't buried in this same place."

"You must open your heart," the minister said to me.

"Why?" I asked. "What else can happen to me? My father is dead."

"You should give thanks for your life, Eric," he said.

"For my life?" I asked bitterly. "What is there about my life to be thankful for?"

Before he could say anything else, I ran off to follow Mr. Fletcher. As I walked beside him, I looked up into his eyes. For just a minute at the cantina they had brightened. Now they were cold and distant again.

"I wish you'd stay awhile," I said. "Not for a long time, just long enough to show me some things. Just long enough to teach me to shoot deer for food this winter."

"Son, it's not deer you want to shoot, is it?" he asked.

"No," I said, frowning. "Somebody's got to kill Dunstan."

"Not you," he said, saying it with a finality that ended our conversation.

As we walked back into town, Corby Johnson stepped out and blocked our path.

"You Fletcher?" Johnson asked.

"Wrong time and place, Johnson," Fletcher said. "Man's hardly cold in the ground. Got to respect the spirits of the dead."

"To give you a chance to weasel your way out of town, you mean," Johnson said.

"Johnson, you go back and tell Dunstan to leave it be. He may start running out of guns," Fletcher told him.

"You know me?" Johnson asked, putting his left hand on his hip but keeping his gun hand loose and ready.

"Saw you in Abilene a year ago," Fletcher said. "You were with the Texas cattle drive. You shot a man that day 'cause you didn't like the way he was laughing."

"I remember," Johnson said. "That was a spell back. You got a memory, Fletcher. Better than me. I don't remember anyone like you. 'Course you might've had a bath back then."

"Heard you'd gotten mouthy," Fletcher said.

"A hair faster, too," Johnson said. "I killed Hank Zachary in Dodge last spring."

"Zachary was old," Fletcher said. "He had too much to lose. I don't have that problem. And I could shoot your eyes out before you hit the ground."

"Might be interesting to find out," Johnson said. "That step faster I am since Abilene might make killing me tough."

"The only step you've taken is a big one closer to the grave, Johnson," Fletcher told him.

"When and where, Fletcher?" Johnson asked.

"Just you, or is Kincaid in on this?" Fletcher asked.

"I'd think one gun'd be more than enough to take care of an old man like you," Johnson said, laughing.

"In front of the saloon, noon tomorrow," Fletcher said.

"You wouldn't be leaving tonight, now would you?" Johnson asked.

"He'll be here," I said, stepping out from behind Fletcher. "We'll keep the undertaker awful busy with you."

"I'll tend to you later, kid," Johnson said, walking off.

As Johnson disappeared, Fletcher took my arm and turned me around.

70

"Boy, don't you ever run your mouth off about me. I talk for myself. When I need somebody to speak my piece for me, I won't go looking for no runt kid like you."

I shook myself free and backed away from him. My eyes were full of pain, and I looked down at my toes.

"I didn't mean anything," I said. "I just wanted you to know I was with you. I'm proud of you. You stood up to him. You'll show him tomorrow. You'll show all of them!"

"I may be going to my grave tomorrow," he said. "I'm in no mood for talk. Is there a bathhouse in this town?"

"Only place to get a bath is the hotel," I said. "They've got one in the back of the saloon, too, but Dunstan owns the place."

"You'd think a man could get a bath before he goes to kill a man. Shows poor manners to gun down a man when you smell like pig slop."

"We've got a tub at our place," I said. "I can heat water. We've got room for you. My brother Willie can sleep on a blanket on the floor. You can have his bed."

"You got a barn?" Fletcher asked, spitting on the ground.

"Sure," I said.

"Get my horse and meet me at the railroad depot. I've got a trunk to get. I can sleep in the barn."

"But you said . . ."

"Never mind what I said. Get my horse."

"Yes, sir," I said, heading for the stable.

As I saddled the horse, I glanced at Mr. Roderick.

"Mr. Fletcher's going to take Johnson tomorrow," I said. "After that the rest of them will be riding out."

"Johnson's pretty fast," Mr. Roderick told me. "It

71

may not turn out the way you want it to."

"No, Fletcher'll kill them, kill them all. He has to," I said, leading the stallion out of the stable.

When I met Fletcher at the station, he lifted the trunk onto the saddle and tied it securely. Then he led the horse down the road.

"How far to your place?" Fletcher asked me.

"Maybe a mile," I said. "It's a pretty easy walk."

"You born here, Eric?" he asked as we walked.

"No, I was born in Texas," I told him.

"Texas?" he asked.

"Jacksboro," I said. "My great-grandfather fought and died in the war against Mexico for independence. I still have two uncles and some cousins back there. They live on a big ranch by the Brazos River."

"I know the Brazos," Fletcher told me. "Used to hunt there when I was young. Then the war came, and everything changed for me."

"You went to the war?" I asked.

"Yeah," he said, frowning. "Never came back, though. War changes a man."

"How?" I asked.

"Well, son, death gets to be an everyday kind of a thing. You see so many men die it gets to where it doesn't matter anymore. You don't take killing and dying too much to heart. Once you get to the point where dying doesn't matter, then you're a man who scares people."

"Scares people?" I asked.

"Most men figure the other man's just as scared as he is. Deep down they know there's a chance they may die. No matter how quick they are, there's always something that can happen. A gun misfires, the sights are wrong on your gun, you slip just a bit.

"One man's pretty much the same as another, you know. When two fast guns square off, one or the

72

other can get himself killed. If you think even a little about it being you, you lose your edge. That one fraction of a second's gone, and you end up the one who's dead."

"Hunt didn't think he could lose," I said.

"Hunt was a fool," he said. "He didn't take me seriously. Once you put that gun in a man's hand, you'd better pay some mind to him."

We walked along in silence for several minutes. Then I saw our farm, and I pointed to it excitedly.

"That's it!" I shouted. "What do you think?"

"Seems a nice enough place," he said. "Too much fence, though. Never cared for fences. They take the world and slice it into little pieces. The Indians never claimed to own the land. They never put their name on it. Only the white man does that.

"Never did understand why people put such value to a place. I been here and there. Some places I liked better than others. But when it comes right down to it, one place is just about as good as another."

"But belonging's important," I said. "You have to know where you come from. None of this was here when we came. Papa built it all."

"You figure people are going to remember that in a hundred years?" he asked. "No one's going to care."

"I will," I said.

When we got the horse put away, I helped Fletcher carry his trunk to a corner. Then I looked at him intently.

"Would you come somewhere with me?" I asked. "Maybe then you'll understand why it's important to belong somewhere."

"All right, son," he said. "It isn't far, is it?"

"No, sir," I said.

We walked out past the barn and made our way to the hill where Papa was buried.

"A graveyard?" he asked.

"Yes," I said, kneeling down beside the picket fence. "There are three crosses."

"One's your father," he said. "The others?"

"My brother Michael and my sister Elsa," I said. "Elsa was only a baby. It's hard to know a baby. Michael was three. He was always smiling and laughing and running around. He got into my things all the time, but it didn't matter. I used to hold him on my lap.

"I miss them. I loved them. Sometimes I'd sit out here and talk to Papa about it. I wish he was here now."

"Sooner or later a man has to stand up on his own," the man told me. "Sometimes it seems early, but you'll be stronger in the long run for it."

"That's what Mama used to say. Lately she's been talking about sending me to Texas. I've got things to do here, though."

"Let's go, son," he said. "You've been around too many graves today."

"Yes, sir," I said, following him back to the barn.

"Tell me about your family," he said.

"There's Mama. She's pretty for a woman who's had a hard life. Then my brothers Tom and Willie. Tom's eleven. Willie's just eight."

"Tell me about them," he said.

"Tom's tall and thin," I said. "He's just about an inch shorter than me. He works real hard, and you can count on him for things."

"And the young one," Fletcher said, swallowing. "Willie. What's he like?"

"Full of fire," I said, laughing. "Willie's like a tornado. He's everywhere at once. He never runs out of energy. He's got a quiet side to him, though. Mama calls it sensitive. Sometimes Willie will come over to me and talk about things a kid like him shouldn't be thinking about."

"He's like you then," Fletcher said.

"I guess," I said.

"You'd best go tell your mother that I'm here. When you get around to it, that bath would be mighty nice."

"Yes, sir," I said. "I'll get to it in a flash."

We went our separate ways then. I walked to the house, and he very slowly made his way to the barn.

IX

"Hey, Eric, where've you been?" Tom asked me as I walked into the house. "Mama's been worrying about you."

"She's all right, isn't she?" I asked.

"Sure," Tom said. "She got up and walked around some. The fever broke. She said you were going to kill a chicken for supper. Are we really going to eat fried chicken?"

"Yeah," I said. "That'll beat turnip soup, won't it?"

"I'll tell Willie," Tom said. "He's cleaning Mama's room."

"I'll tell Willie," I said. "I've got to tell Mama something."

"What?" Tom asked.

"I brought a man home," I said. "I want him to stay, Tom. He's in the barn. I told him we'd fix him a bath and let him sleep here."

"You never brought a man home before. What's going on?" Tom asked.

"He shot Tripp Hunt," I told Tom. "Put a bullet

76

right in his head. Killed him. I saw the whole thing."

"He's that fast?" Tom asked.

"You should see him," I said. "He's quick as lightning. He didn't flinch. You know Hunt. Hunt barely got his gun out of the holster. I never saw anybody so fast."

"He killed Hunt? Won't Dunstan come for him?"

"He's going into town tomorrow to fight Corby Johnson. Before he's through, Dunstan will be packing his bags."

"Eric, what kind of man is he? Is he a sheriff?"

"Not that," I said. "He's a little scary. After he shot Hunt, he went back to the bar and finished his beer. His eyes are weird. There's something about him that sends shivers up your backbone."

"He may be worse than Dunstan," Tom said.

"No," I said, walking past him to Mama's room. "And don't say anything about this to Mama. Or Willie. Willie's got a mouth as big as Texas."

"Sure," Tom said. "I'll start the water to boiling."

"Good," I said.

Mama had gotten out of bed. Her hair was unkempt, and she looked pale as death, but her smile had returned.

"Did you send the wire?" she asked.

"Yes, ma'am," I said.

"Was there any trouble?"

"A little," I said, trying to hide the truth.

"Willie," she said to my little brother, taking his hand, "run and help Tom a minute."

Willie set down the clean sheets and raced off out the door. He hated cleaning, so he was glad to be freed from his duties.

"Tell me everything, Eric," she said.

"Well, Mama, I got the wire sent. Then that man Ryan stopped me. He tossed me around, kicked me, laughed about Papa."

"And what did you do?" she asked.

"I got his gun," I told her. "Mama, I was really scared. I thought they were going to kill me. Then this stranger came over. He told me to give him the gun."

"What sort of stranger?"

"Later, Mama. Anyway, the stranger threw the gun into the watering trough and told the men to leave me be. Then he paid me to tend his horse."

"You shouldn't trust strangers, Eric Sheidler," she said. "I've taught you better."

"Mama, none of the men in town did anything. They would have just stood there and let them kill me."

"They wouldn't have killed you, Eric," she said, laughing.

"They killed Papa," I said, staring at her with fire in my eyes.

"There's more to this," she said. "Tell me."

"They wouldn't let the man stay in town. He helped me, and Dunstan's men are after him. I invited him to stay with us."

"You sure that's all?" she asked. "It's hard to believe Dunstan would send men after a man for helping a little boy."

"I wish you'd quit calling me a little boy," I said.

"Sorry," she said. "It's just you look so awful little right this minute. Tell the man he's welcome to stay to supper. He can stay the night. But tomorrow it'd be best if he'd move on."

"But, Mama . . ."

"You can't trust strangers, Eric," she said. "And if Dunstan is after him, he won't be safe here. Neither will we."

"Yes, ma'am," I said, walking away from her.

Tom and I poured the hot water into two buckets and carried it to the barn. Then we brought the bathtub back behind a horse stall. It took only a minute to fill the tub. Then Willie ran over with a brick of soap.

"We've got the bath ready, Mr. Fletcher," I told him.

"Good boy," he said.

"Mr. Fletcher, these are my brothers," I said. "Tom, Willie, this is Mr. Fletcher."

"Glad to meet you, sir," Tom said.

"Hello," Willie said shyly.

"You boys taking good care of your mother?" he asked.

"Yes, sir," we said together.

"Thanks for the bath, son," he said to me. "I'll be in to dinner shortly."

"Yes, sir," I said, leading my brothers to the chicken coop.

"Can't we stay and watch?" Tom asked. "I'll bet he's got bullet holes all in him."

"Yeah, can't we watch, Eric?" Willie asked.

"A man wants his privacy," I said.

"Papa never sent us away," Tom said.

"That's different," I said. "That's family. Besides, do you want him to get mad and plug you full of holes?"

"You think he'd do that?" Willie asked, hiding behind me.

"Can't ever tell," I said. "We've got to get the chicken."

Tom was better at catching chickens than I was, so he ran inside the coop and hauled out a big fat hen. I grabbed it by the neck and jerked the way Papa had shown me. The bird went limp, and I carried it to the chopping block.

79

"You do the skinning," I told Tom. "I'm going down to get some onions."

"No turnips, Eric," Tom said, pleading. "I don't ever want to see another turnip."

"Not until tomorrow," I said, laughing. "Mama says she has lots of ways of making turnips taste good."

"She must be some kind of witch," Tom said. "Don't see any other way to make a turnip taste good."

I laughed at him, then disappeared behind the barn. In a few minutes I reappeared with a handful of onions. Tom and Willie had just about plucked all the feathers from the chicken, so I carried the onions into the house. They followed with the chicken.

I gutted the bird and began slicing off the different parts. Tom and Willie both liked legs, and I thought more than once it would have been a lot easier if chickens came with four legs instead of two. But that was life.

"You want me to do that?" Mama asked me as I got out a tin of flour.

"You feel like it?" I asked. "It's mighty hot."

"You go tend to your visitor. I'm the cook around here."

"Thanks, Mama," I said. "That's sure going to make things easier. I'm not much of a chicken cook."

"You do just fine," she said. "Still, a woman's touch seems to have a little magic to it."

"Yes, ma'am," I said, running out the door.

"Mama's going to cook supper," I told my brothers.

"Can we watch the man now?" Tom asked.

"No," I told them. "You go in and straighten things up in the house. I'll see if he needs anything. You stay out of his way, see?"

"Sure, Eric," Tom said, dragging Willie along with him into the house.

When I got to the barn, Fletcher was cleaning his gun. He had a different pair of buckskin trousers on, and his skin was lighter than before. His shoulders were still bare, and I noticed they were younger than I'd thought. His face was brighter, too, and I saw for the first time that his hair was light like mine.

"Eric, you don't suppose your father had a razor around, do you?" he asked as I walked over. "I'd sure like to be a bit more presentable to your mother."

"Yes, sir," I said. "I tried it out last week myself. Wasn't much of anything to cut, but I tried it anyway. Seems like a man should shave now and again."

"Seems like," he said, trying not to laugh at me.

I found the razor, then led him to the little basin in the back of the barn.

"We had a hired man who lived here once," I said. "We put out this looking glass and basin for him. I come out here sometimes and . . . you know . . . pretend."

"Did the same myself," he said. "Now let me get at this."

I left him to his shaving and sat down beside his trunk. My eyes were glued on him. I watched his long thin fingers guide the razor across his cheeks, erasing soap and whiskers.

"Bring me a bucket of that warm bath water," he said. "Always use hot water when you shave, son."

"Yes, sir," I said, fetching the water.

I poured the bath water into the basin and watched him finish the job. When he turned around, I was surprised. He looked like a different man. His chin was clean. Only a dark brown mustache and side-burns were left of his beard.

"Do you dress for supper?" he asked.

81

"Well, we don't go naked," I said. "Papa never wore his Sunday clothes, though."

"Then hand me that cotton shirt, son, the one on top of my trunk," he told me.

"Yes, sir," I said.

I took the shirt off the trunk and handed it to him. He slipped it over his head, and I watched it take shape over his strong shoulders.

"Bath makes for a different man, son," he said, slapping me on the back. "I feel like riding after some buffalo."

"Sometimes buffalo still come to the east range," I said. "Papa and Mr. Hazard once rode after them. They killed a bull. Mr. Hazard has the hide on his wall. Papa kept the horns. They're in his room."

"Lots of things change," Fletcher said sadly. "They call it civilization."

I stared at the faraway look in his eyes.

"I believe I smell fried chicken," he said. "How about we have a go at some of it?"

"That'd be just about fine," I said. "It's this way."

We walked in and sat down at the table with Tom and Willie. My brothers were as surprised as I'd been at the change in the man. Mama smiled at him as she sat down.

"Mr. Fletcher, this is my mother, Mrs. Sheidler," I said.

"I'm obliged to you for having me to supper, ma'am," Fletcher said, staring at Mama.

"You're welcome, Mr. Fletcher," she said. "You're welcome to what's ours. I want to thank you for seeing Eric didn't get hurt in town."

"Wasn't much at all," he said, reaching for the chicken.

I nudged him in the side, then shook my head. He pulled back his hand, and Mama's frown lifted.

"Eric, would you return thanks for us tonight?" she asked in a way that left me no choice.

"Yes, ma'am," I said, frowning. "Lord, bless this food and this company. Amen."

"Amen," Tom and Willie echoed.

"I would've thought you could come up with something a little more imaginative, Eric Sheidler, what with company and all," Mama said.

"I imagine, ma'am, that God understands a boy's hunger," Fletcher said, sharing a smile with Mama.

"I suppose He does, Mr. Fletcher," she said, laughing for the first time in a very long while.

As we busied ourselves eating the chicken and potatoes and homemade biscuits, I could tell we'd won Fletcher over to us. He kept looking at Mama with a strange kind of emptiness in his eyes. And he'd watch nearly everything Willie did.

"Tell us about yourself, Mr. Fletcher," Mama said. "What's your business in the Colorado Territory?"

"I don't really know if I have a business, ma'am," he said. "I just wander here and there, staying as long as I feel like it, leaving when I grow tired of things."

"And you have no family?" Mama asked.

"Lost 'em all in the war," he said.

"I'm sorry," she said. "I lost my father. My mother died of the cholera back home. Of course, I was a grown woman then, but I know how hard it can be. I had a younger brother about Eric's age, and I know he had a hard time. He stayed with my husband and me in Jacksboro until he was old enough to start clerking. Now he's a lawyer."

"Fine profession," Fletcher said.

"He writes me every year on my birthday," I said. "Tom and Willie, too."

"Do you ever miss your family?" Mama asked Fletcher.

"Well, I never took much of anybody to heart," Fletcher said, his eyes growing a little moist. "There never was anybody very special, you see. The kind of man I am, a woman finds it hard to feel close to."

"I don't see why," Mama said.

"Didn't your boy tell you what happened in town?" Fletcher asked. "About Hunt?"

"Tripp Hunt?" Mama asked, standing up. "No, he didn't."

"Then I imagine I'm here under false colors, ma'am," he said, frowning. "I was forced to kill this Hunt today. I tell you right here and now that it was a fair fight, ma'am, but I know how a woman feels about having a killer under her roof."

"Why didn't you tell me, Eric?" she asked.

"I was afraid you'd be angry," I said. "Mama, Corby Johnson's called him out. It seemed like the least we should do was give him a place to sleep and a bath."

"I've never turned away a stranger in need," Mama said. "But I believe that if God smiles on you tomorrow, sir, and you are not killed, you should get on your horse and ride away from here."

"That's my plan, ma'am," Fletcher said.

"I know the boys would be happy to give up their room for you tonight. They can put clean linen on the bed, and . . ."

"Ma'am, I appreciate what you're saying, but I'd just as soon take that spot in the barn. I'm not used to having other people around, and if Dunstan has anything in mind for me, I'd rather have it happen where the boys aren't in the way."

"You have nothing to fear tonight," she said. "Mr. Dunstan is quite consistent in these matters. He'll let his hired gunmen do his handywork tomorrow."

"Yes, ma'am," Fletcher said. "I imagine you're

84

right. But I'd still like to take the barn."

"You can have my bed," Willie said. "Michael wouldn't mind."

"I think maybe Mr. Fletcher would like some peace and quiet," I said. "Three of us might be tough to take."

After dinner I sat with Tom on the porch and looked into the clear sky overhead. The sun was just settling into the mountains far to the west.

"He'll kill Johnson tomorrow," I said. "I know he will."

"And then he'll leave," Tom said. "A man like that never stays too long in one place. He said so himself."

"Did you see how he looked at Mama?" I asked. "He'll stay."

"Eric, I hope he leaves," Tom said. "He scares me. He says a lot of words, but they don't mean anything. He never did say where he was from or what he's doing here."

"Tom, he's a gunfighter," I said. "He goes from one town to the next, looking for work."

"But why come here?" Tom asked.

"He came to get his trunk at the station," I said.

"Why here?" Tom asked. "Why not Pueblo?"

"I don't know," I said.

"You'd better find out," Tom told me. "Get a look in that trunk. Check him out, Eric. There's something scary about him being here."

As Tom walked off, Fletcher walked out from the barn smoking a long cigar. It was the expensive kind Sheriff Campbell used to smoke.

I walked over to him, and we stood together in front of the house a few minutes before he spoke.

"Do you have a picture of your father, Eric?" he asked. "Maybe one of him and your mother together."

"There's one on the wall," I said. "I'll show you." We walked inside, and I showed him the photograph.

"That isn't Jacksboro," he said, pointing to the small buildings in the background.

"I know," I said. "Papa told me where it was once. Mama was born on a ranch, you know. They got married in a little town near the ranch. Then they moved to Jacksboro."

"You remember the name of the town?" he asked.

"No," I said, surprised he was interested. "It was before I was born."

"Think hard, son," he told me. "Try to remember."

"Sure," I said, seeing how white his face had become. He was breathing heavily. It seemed the question was very important.

"It was something like Pablo. I remember Papa said it meant pointed stick in Spanish," I said.

"Not white," he said, breathing easier. "Painted. Palo Pinto. It's just south of the Brazos."

"That's it!" I said. "You've been there?"

"Yes," he said.

"You knew Mama there, didn't you?" I said. "I knew it. I could see it in your eyes at supper."

"Don't you say one word about any of this," he told me.

"Why not?" I asked.

"You hear me, Eric?" he asked, squeezing my arm until it hurt. "Not a word, promise?"

"All right," I said, yanking my arm away from him.

"A man isn't anything unless he keeps his promises," the man said. "You know that?"

"I'll keep my promise," I said. "I won't say anything."

"Good," he said. "Have a good night then, son. I'll be seeing you in the morning."

"Yes, sir," I said, watching him disappear out the door.

X

We had a quiet breakfast that next morning. Mama fixed flapjacks, and we gobbled them up. Fletcher sat quietly and only nibbled at his breakfast.

"I hope the food is all right, Mr. Fletcher," Mama said to him.

"Oh, it is, ma'am," the man said. "I just seem to have a lot on my mind."

His words hung a cloud of gloom over the table. Not another word was spoken, and even Willie seemed to lose his appetite. I never knew anything to stop his mouth from taking in flapjacks.

When Mama dismissed us, I followed Fletcher out to the barn. I sat down beside his trunk and watched him shave.

"You suppose you could manage some bath water for me again this morning?" he asked. "A man should look his best when . . . when he's . . ."

"Yes, sir," I said. "I know what you mean."

I returned a short while later with the buckets of hot water. As I poured the water into the tub, I felt a hand on my shoulder. I turned and stared at Fletcher's face. There was something new in his eyes.

"Your bath's ready," I said.

"Thanks," he said, unbuttoning his shirt. "I want you to know, Eric, no matter how this comes out, it's been nice being here with your family."

"Must be pretty lonely drifting around, huh?" I asked.

"Sometimes," he said. "Sometimes I wonder why I didn't find myself a wife, have a few kids, raise some potatoes or corn. But I've never been one to settle down. I guess a man just makes his way the best he can. Doesn't do any good to question things."

"Yes, sir," I said.

He slipped into the tub, and I handed him a square of soap. He began scrubbing himself, and I found myself watching him. All of what I'd said to Tom and Willie couldn't ward off my curiosity.

His shoulders and chest were taut as a good rope, and you could tell he was a man who'd not led a gentle life. There were two spots on his chest with thin red scars. I'd seen bullet scars before. These were the same. The rest of the man's chest was covered by fine, curly brown hair.

"The one on my arm I got from a Comanche war lance," he said, following my eyes. "I was thirteen years old. It was a kind of game between me and a friend of mine, the son of a chief. He won," Fletcher said, laughing, "but I got the scar because of it. It made me sort of a brother to the Comanche."

"Was that back in Texas?" I asked. "When you knew Mama?"

"I told you not to talk about that," he said. "That was another man, not me."

"She'd want to know," I said. "I think maybe she recognized you."

"Couldn't have," he said. "You keep quiet about this, hear?"

"Yes, sir," I said.

89

I looked the rest of him over. There were two other bullet scars on his back, a fifth on his side. And there were wicked-looking scars across his belly that could only have been caused by cavalry sabers.

When he stood up, I saw there were more saber scars on his legs. There was also a jagged scar on his hip that might have been put there by a knife. He was a man who'd known pain, who'd faced death.

As Fletcher dried himself, Tom and Willie peeked in through the door. I turned to chase them off, but Fletcher stopped me.

"Let them come in," he told me.

Tom walked over and felt the leather of Fletcher's gunbelt.

"Have you killed many men, Mr. Fletcher?" Tom asked.

"Too many," he answered. "I lost count a good while back."

"You mean you've killed so many men you don't even remember how many?" Tom asked.

"I only remember their faces, not how many," the man said.

"Gosh," Willie said, sitting down at the man's feet. "I'll bet you could kill even Mr. Dunstan."

"Won't have to," Fletcher said. "I expect Eric's already told you I'm leaving when I finish with Johnson."

I looked at him with surprise, but he nodded to me. I just walked away.

"Eric, look in my trunk and see if you can find my good white shirt, the one with the lace down the front," he said to me.

"Lace?" I asked.

"Picked it up down in New Orleans," he explained. "It's a fine shirt."

"Yes, sir," I said, lifting the lid of the trunk.

The inside was stuffed with all sorts of things. There were several pistols, five cartridge boxes, a couple of books and several leather pouches.

"Find it?" he asked.

"Still looking," I said.

As I ran my fingers through the stacks of clothing. I heard something jingle. It was the pouches. I felt the side of one of them. They were filled with coins.

Looking behind me to make sure no one was watching, I opened the pouch up and saw it contained twenty dollar gold pieces. There was a small fortune in the trunk. Then I saw at last the shirt he was talking about. I held it up, smoothing out the wrinkles.

"Is this it?" I asked.

"That's the one," he told me.

I handed it to him, and he slipped it over his bare shoulders.

"It's a fine-looking shirt, Mr. Fletcher," Tom said.

"Hand me those dark blue britches," Fletcher told me then. "The ones without the stripe."

"Here," I said, handing him the trousers.

Fletcher put on the pants and pulled them tight. He then took out a wide leather belt and fastened it around his waist.

"Fit as a fiddle," he said, doing the first of several deep knee bends. "Help me with my boots. First hand me my stockings, the red ones."

I tossed them to him, and he snatched them out of the air quick as a cat. Then I helped him put on the boots which I'd shined the night before so that they sparkled in the bright morning sunlight.

"Well, boys, what do you think?" Fletcher asked, buckling on his gunbelt.

"Gosh," Willie said, stepping back. "That's a mighty fine outfit, Mr. Fletcher."

"Mighty fine," Tom said.

"A man should dress to go to battle," Fletcher said, smiling. "Now you two boys," he said, pointing to Tom and Willie, "can run along and tend to your chores. When you turn out your horses, you might take mine along."

"Sure," Tom said. "Come on, Willie."

"They're good boys," Fletcher told me after they'd left.

"Yes, sir," I said. "They've taken a liking to you. Pretty soon they'll be as bad about hanging around you as I am."

"They'll never have that chance," he said.

I looked up at him with a hundred questions on my lips. I wanted to know who he was, where he'd come from, how come he knew Mama. But I just sat there.

"Something bothering you, son?" he asked.

"Yes," I said, looking down. "How come the letters on the inside of the trunk say W.D.?"

"Well, the trunk once belonged to a friend of mine," he explained. "Somebody I knew back in Texas. We fought together in the war. He was killed in Virginia. I took the trunk, though. I'd always liked it, and he would have wanted me to have it."

I sat down beside him, and he studied my face.

"There's something else," he said at last. "What is it?"

"I saw the leather pouches," I told him.

"You look inside them?" he asked.

"Yes, sir," I said. "There's a lot of money there."

"Some," he said.

"Where'd you get so much money?" I asked. "Killing people?"

"That what you think?" he asked.

"I don't know what to think," I said. "I know for

sure you're not what you say you are. You can tell me. You can trust me."

"I know that, son, but it would change things in a way I don't think either one of us could handle just now. The coins I came by honestly. I did some mining up in Montana. There's a book in there with the number of a bank account up in Denver. There's a lot more money there."

"Why tell me?" I asked.

"There's a reason, take it at that. If something happens in town and I don't make it back here, I want you to take the coins and the book to your mother. Tell her to look through the trunk. She'll know everything when she looks at the things in there.

"But promise me this, Eric. Don't tell her a thing if I come back. You understand?"

"You're going to tell her yourself, huh?"

"Don't know," he said. "If I thought it'd do you, any of you one ounce of good, then I'd explain. Wouldn't, though."

"How can you be sure?" I asked.

"I know," he said.

He locked up the trunk and put the key in his pocket. Then he led the way into town. As we walked, he whistled to himself. The sound floated along through the air, and it broke the tension.

"Who are you?" I asked him as we walked. "Really, I mean. Do you have a name?"

"Got several," he said. "Fletcher's one of them. You might have heard some of them. But a name's only a word. You get a reputation, and you throw the old name away."

"Don't people recognize you?" I asked.

"Only the ones you get real close to," he said. "I haven't got close to many lately. I let my beard grow

93

sometimes. Then I shave my mustache. Sometimes I grow my hair long. I dress this way and that.

"When they get to know you too well, you get a big rep. Then every kid from here to Santa Fe goes looking for you. Art Danby once shot six kids under twenty in one week down on the Cimarron."

"Were you out there?" I asked. "You seem to know a lot about it."

"I was there awhile," he said.

"They hired you to kill men," I said, frowning.

"Listen to just this one thing, Eric," he said. "Nobody ever gave me money to kill a man. Nobody ever paid me to shoot someone. I got paid for riding fencelines, for defending my boss, for herding cattle."

"It was a range war," I said. "If you kill men when somebody pays you, it's the same thing."

"No, Eric, it's not, not anymore than serving in the army is. Somebody's paying you to fight for them. I never killed a man up there that didn't ask to get killed. I never shot a man with kids, and I never shot one that was riding away.

"I used to be quite a man of conscience. I used to have a lot of rules. Now I don't have any except to stay alive. If somebody pushes too hard, then he's going to die."

I looked into the coldness that came into his eyes. I watched the way he set his jaw. There was no room for compromise in his life now. The other man yielded, or somebody died.

XI

It was almost noon when we reached town. I walked beside Fletcher as he approached the saloon. Then as we passed the feed store, I stopped. There was a wooden sign with Dunstan's name on it nailed over the door of the store where Papa had painted SHEIDLER'S FEED STORE.

"You'd best stay here," Fletcher said, pushing me toward the store.

"I want to go with you," I told him.

"Wouldn't be much point to that, now would there?" he asked me. "You remember what I told you about the trunk?"

"Yes, sir," I said, sighing.

As Fletcher walked on to the saloon, I sat down on the wooden bench Papa had made for me. It was hard and splintery, but it was all I had left of Papa's love. I felt comfortable there.

Across the street a great deal of laughter was coming from the saloon. Suddenly someone yelled out, and the saloon grew quiet. Then Corby Johnson walked out of the swinging doors, smoking a cigar and grinning.

"Well, here at last," Johnson said, spitting out the cigar. "Got yourself a bath I see. Sure do look pretty. Hey, boys," Johnson said to the men in the saloon, "he sure does look pretty. Got all dressed up like he was going to be buried. I'd sure hate to disappoint folks. Does seem a shame to stain such a pretty white shirt, though."

Kincaid walked out and sat on the porch next to Johnson. Then Ryan and a couple of Dustan's errand boys came out, too. Everyone else scattered. I was the only one left on my side of the street.

"They say you like to talk a man to sleep, Johnson," Fletcher said. "They say you like to get your back to the sun and shoot a blind man. But I don't shoot with my eyes, Johnson. I use my nose. I can smell you, Johnson. There's a smell of death to you today."

"Your death," Johnson said, laughing.

"You want to come on out here and let's get this over with. I've got a train to catch this afternoon."

"Only place you got to go is straight to hell, mister," Johnson said. "Tripp Hunt was a friend of mine."

"Oh, now let's not start that kind of talk, Johnson," Fletcher said. "You and Hunt never had a friend in your whole life. Me, neither. We're the last of a kind, you and me. We don't want any friends."

"I hear you got friends out of town," Johnson said. "Heard there's a widow out there who wasn't exactly lonely last night."

I stood up and started to run out into the street, but something stopped me. It was the cold glance cast my way by Fletcher.

96

"What's this kid to you, anyway?" Johnson went on saying. "We never gave much mind to him. Now I guess we'd best clean out the whole nest. They say when a bird dies, the other birds come down to the nest and throw all the little ones out. They die of hunger or get pecked to death. Birds might have a good idea. I hear Dunstan's got some fine things planned for that boy and his little brothers. Some of them Comanches down to the south use white boys for slaves."

"Come on, Johnson," Fletcher said, spitting on the ground in front of him. "This is beginning to get downright tiresome. Let's get it over with. I haven't got all day."

"Getting nervous?" Johnson asked. "Wouldn't want to hurry things. Reminds me of something my pa said once. It seems this . . ."

Quick as a flash Johnson reached for his gun. Just as Johnson's gun leveled off, a single shot rang out. The sentence was never finished. A spot of red appeared on Johnson's shirt, and the man dropped to his knees. The gun fell from Johnson's fingers, and his eyes became cloudy.

I ran over beside Fletcher. We walked together to where Johnson lay.

"Who . . . are . . . you?" Johnson gasped as the blood poured forth from the hole in his chest.

"Some call me Fletcher," Fletcher said.

"No," Johnson said, looking at him with confusion. "Something else. On the Cimarron. I saw you. You . . ."

But Johnson spoke no more than that. His eyes went blank, and he toppled over face down in the dusty street.

"Corby?" Kincaid screamed out, rushing into

97

the street.

"You're too late, Kincaid," Fletcher said. "Johnson's dead."

"Then so are you," said Kincaid, backing away.

I dove to the ground a second before two shots rang out. The first tore into the ground beside my feet. The other knocked Kincaid back against the post in front of the saloon. Blood streamed down Kincaid's forehead, and the gunman fell down like a stuffed rag doll.

"Anybody else?" Fletcher asked, waving his pistol at the men standing in the door of the saloon. "Anybody else want to die today?"

Two of the men threw their arms in the air, and the others scrambled inside the saloon.

"Get them to the undertaker," Fletcher said to the men with their arms in the air. "Then get out of town. Go somewhere where there's no dying to be done."

Fletcher walked over to me and pulled me to my feet.

"Don't you ever come charging down there like that again," he told me. "It's the best way I know to get yourself killed. I told you yesterday Johnson and Kincaid were a pair. Now maybe they can get graves next to each other."

"You got them both," I said. "Now there's nobody left except Dunstan."

"There's always somebody left, Eric," he said. "Always."

I followed him to the ticket office of the railroad. Mr. Ames, the ticket agent, turned to him and smiled.

"What's your pleasure, sir?" Mr. Ames asked.

"One ticket west," Fletcher said.

"Where to?" Mr. Ames asked.

"Doesn't matter," Fletcher told him.

"Well, sir, I can tell you right now there won't be a train heading anywhere west for two days," Mr. Ames said.

"Then east," Fletcher said.

"Train headed for Johnson City tomorrow morning," the ticket agent said. "Might be late. Engineer's got a new wife in Pueblo, and sometimes he doesn't get off on time."

"Nothing at all until tomorrow?" Fletcher asked. "Not even a freight?"

"Nothing, mister," Mr. Ames said.

"Well, thanks just the same," Fletcher said.

As we walked away from the ticket office, he turned to me.

"You think if I sent you a wire, you could put that trunk on a freight for me?" he asked. "Think you could do it?"

"Sure," I said. "If Dunstan doesn't steal it."

"Dunstan won't," he told me.

"Then I could do it. You riding out?" I asked.

"Don't see there's much choice," he said. "If I stay, you'll be the one who pays."

"I'll take my chances," I said. "I'm not afraid. Mr. Fletcher, the people would back you. We could get rid of Dunstan. He doesn't have a top gun left."

"Eric, since I've come to this town, you're the only one I've met with any backbone at all. The hotel manager wouldn't even rent me a room. Now you tell me, son, you think he'd risk his life?"

"I guess not," I said.

"You know not," Fletcher said, laughing.

"But you promised to teach me to shoot," I

99

said.

"I did no such thing. That was your promise, not mine. I'm not your father, Eric. I couldn't ever be."

"I don't remember asking you to be," I said, looking at him with anger in my eyes. "It's you who goes around calling me son. I didn't ask you to do that. I thought maybe we were friends. A friend doesn't run out on another friend when they're in trouble. He stands beside him."

"Even if it means getting shot up?" Fletcher asked.

"Yes," I said. "You teach me to shoot, and I'll stand up with you against Dunstan or anybody he hires."

"No, Eric," he told me.

As Fletcher walked boldly through the swinging doors of the saloon, I peered down at the puddles of blood in the street left behind by Johnson and Kincaid.

"Never saw such a cold-blooded man," somebody behind me said. "Not ever."

"He's the devil himself," another said.

"Didn't even bat an eye after killing two men," somebody else said.

"And to do it in front of a boy," said a lady.

"He scares me out of my wits," one man said. "He'd as soon shoot you as look at you."

"Dunstan himself isn't any worse," another woman said.

"Oh yes he is!" I shouted to them. "Dunstan doesn't wait around for a man to draw. Dunstan doesn't even care if a man has a gun. Dunstan doesn't mind shooting a woman or a boy. You didn't even see them. Both of them drew first.

100

And if they'd walked away, there wouldn't've been any fight."

The people mumbled to themselves. I knew they were talking about me, and I hated them for it. Fletcher had been right. Those people would never stand up to Dunstan.

I started walking home. As I passed the cantina, Mitch Ryan jumped out in front of me.

"Mr. Dunstan would like to know all about this Fletcher," Ryan said. "Sure would be a shame for a fine boy like you to get himself all cut up. Why don't you tell us about him?"

Ryan then took out a big knife and swung it around in his big hand.

"What do you say, boy, the truth?" he asked.

"I don't know anything," I said, backing away.

"Seems to me you might be lying," he said, making a lunge for me with the knife.

I started to run, but one of Ryan's friends grabbed me. He pinned my arms behind my back, and I kicked out at him.

"Going to get yourself killed, boy," Ryan said, taking the knife and cutting off the top button of my shirt. "You keep squirming, I might just slip."

I froze as he placed his arm against my stomach and sliced off a second button.

"Want to tell me something?" Ryan asked.

"I don't know anything," I said. "He was in the cavalry."

"Now we're getting somewhere," he said, taking his knife and ripping my shirt open to my waist.

"You ever seen how the Indians carve up a boy?" he asked.

"No," I said, shaking.

"Well, they start at the center of the chest like

101

this," he said, taking the knife and lightly breaking the flesh just below my breastbone. Blood trickled down onto my stomach, and I coughed.

"That was just a little sample, boy," Ryan said. "The next cut went across the stomach."

"Come on, Mitch," said one of the other men. "The kid don't know nothing."

"He knows," Ryan said, smiling. "And before we're through, we'll know, too."

As Ryan brought the knife close to my bare stomach, I slammed down my foot on the toes of the man who held me. Then I kicked out at Ryan, catching him on the left shin.

"Why you little pig!" Ryan said, grabbing my arm. "I'll teach you!"

Ryan reached back and hit me across the face. My eyes closed, and I could feel blood in my mouth. I staggered, then fell down.

"Now you've gone and done it, Mitch," one of the others said. "You went and knocked him out. Won't get anything out of him now."

"Well, maybe now we should pay a little visit to old lady Sheidler. She might have some answers," Ryan said.

I tried to get to my feet, but I was dizzy, and I couldn't make my arms and legs work.

"She wouldn't know anything," one of the men said. "Fletcher's been in town most of the time. No, the kid's the only chance."

"Let's take him to Dunstan," Ryan said. "Let the old man have a go at him."

"If Fletcher finds out we've got the kid, we've had it," one of the men said.

"You running short on guts, Faulks?" Ryan asked.

"You know it," the man named Faulks said. "Here comes Fletcher now."

I could hear their footsteps disappearing in the distance. Then someone picked me up.

"What happened, Eric?" asked Fletcher as he shook me to my senses. "Who did this to you?"

"Dunstan's men," I mumbled.

I could feel the side of my face aching, and I spit out a mouthful of blood.

"I should have expected this," he said. "Can you walk?"

"Sure," I said, leaning against him.

I walked maybe three steps before falling down. My legs were wobbly, and my head was filled with haze.

"You just take it easy, son," he told me, lifting my body in his strong arms. "It isn't far."

XII

I was plenty scared when I came to. I had an awful swollen spot on the side of my face, and one eye would still only open partway. Looking up, I saw Mama standing over me.

"Mama, am I home?" I asked, sitting up.

"Mr. Fletcher brought you in," she said. "You'd better lie back down awhile."

"I'm all right," I said, shaking my head.

"I was wrong, wasn't I?" she asked.

"About what?" I asked.

"About him," she said. "About Mr. Fletcher. They started in on you."

"Mama, I was scared," I said. "I always thought I was tough like Papa. But when Ryan took out that knife . . ."

"What knife?" she asked.

I looked down at my shirt. The top two buttons were still gone, but the rest of it was fastened here and there. I could see a thin scab where Ryan had cut my chest. Mama hadn't noticed that.

"Oh, it's nothing much," I said. "He pointed this knife at me, and I squirmed away. That's when he hit me."

"Well, that settles one thing," Mama said. "You boys are going to your Uncle Sam. I won't have Dunstan and his men waving knives at you."

I could see she was upset. There wasn't any point in discussing it anymore right then.

"I'm all right now, Mama," I said, sliding my feet over the side of the bed. "I was supposed to see about the meat today."

"Tom rode your horse over to Mr. Franks's place to see about it. Everything's just fine," she told me.

I stood up and looked into her eyes.

"I know you're just trying to get even with me for all those hours you were laid up, but really, I'm fine."

She felt my forehead, then smiled.

"Well, Eric, you look like somebody took after you with a stick, but you don't have any fever. Take care now," Mama said. "And no riding till that bump on your head's gone."

"Yes, ma'am," I said.

I walked past her out of the house and made my way to the barn. Fletcher was lacing a buckskin shirt, showing my brother Willie how it was done.

"Well, I figured you'd be in bed the rest of the day," he said to me. "You missed the funeral and everything."

"Sorry," I said, frowning. "I'm not going to any more funerals," I said. "Except my own."

"Eric, your face is all messed up," Willie told me, running over and looking at it close up. "What happened?"

"I got beat up. Listen, Willie," I told him, "do you suppose you could run and check on the horses?"

"Tom's bringing them in," Willie said. "Mr. Fletcher was showing me how to make a shirt out of a deer's skin."

"Go see after the horses, Willie," Fletcher said.

105

"You always mind your brother now. We'll finish the shirt tomorrow."

"You promise?" Willie asked.

"I promise," Fletcher told him.

Willie flashed his special smile at us, then raced off like a grizzly bear to find Tom.

"You got something you want to say?" Fletcher asked, looking at me.

"Yes," I said. "I wanted to thank you for not telling Mama about the cut on my chest."

"That wasn't for you," he said. "I should have known better than to leave you in town on your own after what happened. They might not have stopped where they did."

"He was going to cut my stomach, but I kicked him," I said. "That's when he hit me. He was trying to get me to tell about you."

"And you wouldn't?"

"I said I didn't know anything. I told them some things I knew didn't matter, like you being in the cavalry. I wouldn't tell them about the other things, the things you made me promise not to."

"Why not?" he asked.

"Because a man doesn't break his promises," I said. "I'm not much of a man, I know. I can't protect myself, much less my family. I suppose that's how Papa felt. But I can at least stand up to them, Mr. Fletcher."

"Only a fool stands still for another man to knock him down, Eric."

"You mean like the Indian who struck you with that war lance when you were thirteen?" I asked.

"That was boys playing games," he said.

"What would you do, run away?"

"Fast as I could," he told me. "You stay alive that way."

"Some alive," I said. "How can you be anything when you're always running? You never build anything."

"Sometimes it's enough to enjoy life, to see all there is to see, to do all there is to do," he told me.

"Not for me," I said. "Maybe it's because you lost your family in the war. If you knew how it was to have Tom and Willie and Mama all depending on you, you'd know you're all wrong about running away. It's hard, Mr. Fletcher, but what happens to me matters to people. They count on me."

Fletcher walked away and sat down for a minute.

"Must be a mighty fine thing to have all the answers when you're so young," he said.

"Yeah," I said, laughing at myself. "Sometimes I get carried away with myself. You haven't gone, though."

"I won't be going now," he said. "That was Ryan's doing. It's not a personal thing between me and Dunstan anymore. It's more than that. It ties in your family, and I won't go off and leave you to pay for my doings."

"Then we're allies," I said, running over to him. "I knew it. Now you can teach me to shoot. I have a pistol, you know."

"This is my battle, son," he said. "Can you handle a rifle?"

"Yes, sir," I said.

"Do you have a Winchester?"

"In the house," I told him. "Papa always kept it there on account of wolves."

"Keep it at your side tonight," he said. "You might have need of it."

"You think they'll come here?" I asked.

"It's what I'd do," he said. "Dunstan is many things. None of them's a fool. He doesn't have a gun he can face me with now. He'll do it another way."

"Maybe we should send Mama away with Tom and Willie?"

"There are two reasons not to. First, I don't think they'd go. You wouldn't. Second, I don't think there's any way you could be sure they could get away safely. If Dunstan found out and got them, they'd be in more danger than they'd ever be here."

"He wouldn't hurt them, would he?"

"He hurt you, didn't he?" Fletcher asked.

I looked at the floor. He'd made his point.

"It's like a war then," I said, trembling. "Well, my family's fought wars before."

"Sleep lightly, Eric," he told me. "You might move the beds away from the windows, too."

"You want to come inside the house?" I asked.

"It's best if I stay in the barn. That way if they come just for me, you'll be pretty safe."

"I'll get the beds moved," I said. "We ought to have steaks for supper tonight."

"A good meal will make us all feel better," he said.

Supper was eaten in silence. Tom brought back the meat, and we all ate well. Mama even seemed to have some appetite. Tom and Willie went out to the barn to watch Fletcher lace the rest of the buckskin shirt, and I loaded two rifles.

"You expect trouble tonight, Eric?" Mama asked as I took down the cartridge box from the high shelf in the front room.

"Mr. Fletcher said Dunstan might send some men," I said.

"Where are you taking the rifles?" she asked.

"To my room," I said. "I figured Tom might be able to fire one of them."

"Tom tries awful hard," she said, "but he's shot a rifle less than you have. You hand me that gun. I

108

shot a wolf out here once when your papa was off in Pueblo."

"I never knew that," I said. "You never talked about it," I told her, wrapping my arm around her waist.

"Well, Eric, it isn't the kind of thing that comes up in polite society," she said, hugging me. "But I was the first child in my family, and Papa always figured girl or boy, a kid should learn to handle a rifle."

"I'll bet you were tough on Indians," I said.

"They were mostly peaceful when I was growing up," she said. "I shot my share of coons, though. I even nailed a cougar when was fifteen."

"Mama, how come we never really know our family?" I asked her. "I mean I talked a lot to Papa, but I feel like we were strangers."

"I don't know, Eric," she said. "I guess it's because a child always sees mostly the good in his folks. He can't really understand the human side. You always look for the best in your family. You don't go looking for the weaknesses. And that's what really makes up most people."

"I guess," I said, feeling her squeeze me.

We were in bed maybe two hours when something woke me. I sat up in the bed. Every part of me concentrated to hear something. At last I heard the clop clop of horses, and I grabbed my pants, took the rifle and shook Tom awake.

"Run in and tell Mama someone's outside," I told him.

"Not naked," Tom said.

"Well, get Willie up, and I'll tell Mama," I said. "You two get on the floor and keep down."

As Tom scrambled into his pants, I raced into Mama's room and tapped her shoulder.

"Mama, somebody's outside," I whispered.

109

"Keep the boys down," she said, taking the second rifle. "Be careful, Eric."

"You, too," I said.

I then ran back to my room and tried to see what was going on.

"They're behind the barn, Eric," Tom told me. "I saw at least three of them."

"I'm going out there," I said.

"You can't," Tom said, holding onto my arm. "You got to guard the house."

"Mama's got a rifle," I said. "Mr. Fletcher can't take on three of them by himself."

Just then a rifle blast shattered the window beside us, and Tom and I hit the floor together. Another shot was fired, and I heard the rifle in Mama's room bark out a reply.

I swung my rifle out the window, brushing aside the shattered glass. A rifle flashed out in front of me, and I fired at the spot. A man yelled something and ran away.

"Hey, Mitch," another shouted, "the house is firing, too. Let's get out of here."

Then two shots rang out from inside the barn. Someone called out. Then there was a series of pistol shots, and a man limped out the front of the barn.

"We got him!" the man screamed.

I looked through the sights of my rifle at the man. I didn't know him, didn't want to recognize him. He was silhouetted in the moonlight, and he made a perfect target. I squeezed the trigger, and the man fell backward against the barn. Then he rolled over onto the ground.

"Let's go!" another man shouted.

A second man jumped on a horse and rode with him. Three horses remained riderless, and I realized Tom had seen only three of them. I jumped through the window and pursued them.

"Run all the way to Dunstan!" I screamed. "Tell him to come back and die himself!"

I walked by the man I'd shot. He was lying on his back, bleeding from one leg and his right shoulder.

"Don't shoot, boy," the man said, looking up at me. "I just came 'cause Dunstan paid me. I'll get out of town, I promise. You'll never see me again."

"Go!" I said, waving at his horse. "Don't ever come back!"

I stepped on his rifle so that he couldn't take it with him, and his face turned white. His shirt was soaked in blood, and he couldn't walk right. He got to his horse, though, and rode off like a prairie fire.

I crept inside the barn, kicking the two bodies near the door to make sure they were dead. Then I saw Fletcher. He was lying on the floor. Around his left leg the straw was stained red. I choked, wanting to throw up.

"Come help me, son," he said. "I took a bullet in my leg."

I ran to him and helped him up.

"Get me to your house," he said. "You suppose your ma can take a bullet out of my hide?"

"Mama's good at doctoring," I said. "You'll see."

As we passed the dead men, I recognized one of them as Mitch Ryan. He was about the last of the men who'd come to town with Dunstan. The others had come later.

"Is your leg bad?" I asked, feeling him lean more on me.

"Not so bad," he said. "I been shot worse."

"Well, you aren't going to ride anywhere now," I said. "This'll keep you around awhile."

"It'll give Dunstan time," he told me.

"I don't understand," I said.

111

"You will," he said. "Looks like you'll be learning to shoot a handgun after all."

I helped him on into the house. Mama had him lie on the kitchen table. She ripped his trouser leg open, then tied a piece of cloth across his thigh above the wound. That stopped the bleeding.

"Eric, get that bottle of spirits from the cabinet. You boys get back to bed," she said, pointing to Tom and Willie.

"Ah, Mama," Tom complained.

"Now!" she shouted.

When I brought the bottle over, Fletcher grabbed it and swallowed about a third of its contents.

"That was for cleaning the wound," Mama told him.

"Just cleaning it out from the inside," he said, laughing. "You ever take a bullet out, ma'am?"

"A few," she said.

"Well, get at it," he said. "I've bled about enough."

I watched as she took out a sharp knife and ran it under the flame from the lamp. Then she splashed some whiskey over both the knife and the wound. Fletcher winced as the whiskey soaked into the wound. Then Mama started cutting.

He was a tough man. I never thought he'd be afraid of anything. He never cried out, but as Mama dug, he suddenly passed out. She pulled the bullet out, then turned to me.

"Get some gunpowder," she said.

"Gunpowder?" I asked.

"Yes," she said. "I can't explain it now. Just get it."

I broke three rifle cartridges apart and poured the powder into my hand. Then I sprinkled it over his wound like she said. Finally she took the hot knife and burned it into the flesh. It turned his leg black and ugly, but there was no more bleeding.

"That seals the broken veins," she said. "Eric, I want you to clean him up now. Then take him and put him in your bed. You won't mind sleeping on the floor, will you?"

"No, Mama," I said.

Actually it took Mama, Tom and me to get him into the bed. Mama then bandaged his leg, binding it tight. Then Tom rolled into bed with Willie, and I spread out a blanket on the floor. I didn't sleep much the rest of the night, though.

XIII

Word of the shootings at our place spread through the countryside like wildfire. All kinds of people stopped by to offer help, and for the first time it seemed like the people of the town might be ready to stand up to Dunstan.

Mostly, though, the people seemed to want Fletcher to get well and finish the job by himself. They told him how brave he was, how wonderful it was to have a man in Whitlow who fought for justice. Behind his back they called him a cold-blooded killer. It riled me.

After the first two days everything in Whitlow changed. The saloon tables were abandoned. The men who'd crowded around Dunstan and his fast guns began disappearing one by one. Dunstan could only keep the mercantile, the bank and the saloon open, and everyone kept expecting Dunstan himself to leave any day.

It took Fletcher two more days after that to get himself mended well enough to ride. Mama had figured it would be the better part of a week, but Fletcher healed faster than any man I'd ever seen.

He hadn't even bled after that first night.

When he walked into breakfast all dressed, we could hardly believe it.

"You going into town to get even with them today?" Willie asked.

"You don't ask a man a question like that," Mama said, scolding Willie. "What Mr. Fletcher does is his own business."

Fletcher laughed, then pulled his chair back a few inches from the table.

"What are your plans for this morning, son?" he asked me.

"I have to check the fence line," I said. "Mr. Hazard sometimes gives us vegetables for it. And we can't let our own cattle wander."

"That's a job for a grown man," Fletcher said, frowning.

"Well, that's me," I said. "At least I'm the closest thing we've got around here."

"You're young to be doing a man's work, Eric," Fletcher said.

"You know how it is," I said to him. "You do what you have to do."

"I know all about that," Fletcher said. "I was just thinking. I'm getting a bit rusty from being laid up. And a man ought to earn his keep. How about me riding out with you?"

"That would be just fine," I said, smiling. "You sure you're up to it?"

"Sure as I ever was about anything," he said.

"Can I come, too?" Tom asked.

"Tom, the cattle have to be moved to the north pasture," Mama said, catching the disappointment that filled my face at the idea of Tom coming along. "You've got your chores to do."

"We could meet you at the creek when we're

finished," I said. "Maybe we could fish and swim a little."

"Could we, Mama?" Tom asked.

"The fish would make for a fine supper," Mama said. "You look after Willie, Tom. See he doesn't stick one of those hooks into his foot again."

"Yes, ma'am," Tom said.

Fletcher and I rode off about mid-morning. The sky was cloudy, and there was a cooling breeze sweeping across the prairie from the north. I found myself watching him as he rode. Papa had been a good horseman, a fine carpenter, a great man. This Fletcher rode like the horse was a part of him, though.

He seemed to be balanced like one of Mama's fine crystal glasses on top of the saddle, light and somehow valuable. But there was nothing delicate about the man. His face was filled with a hardness, a look of contempt for the rest of the world. And when we rode over rough ground, he would wince as his wound was jarred.

The Confederate cavalry hat made him look very military. He was far more like a general than the cavalry commander who'd ridden through town looking for Cheyennes two summers before. There was no fear in Fletcher's eyes, no thought of turning back. Here was a man who rode onward even through the valley of death itself.

As I watched him ride along, he glanced over at me. The coldness in his eyes seemed to leave momentarily, and a faint smile came to his lips. Then, as quickly as it had come, the smile vanished, and the stern face of the gunfighter returned.

"We have to ford this creek back upstream," I said as we reached the creek. "The fence line isn't

116

far now."

"Lead on, son," he told me.

I reined my horse and nudged him to the right. Then we trotted into the creek and splashed our way across.

"Have much trouble with fences out here?" Fletcher asked me.

"Not too much," I said. "We had a small herd of buffalo stampede through here once. They knocked down about fifty yards of the east section, posts and all. It was a real chore to put all those posts back in. We did have buffalo steaks for a week, though."

We shared a brief laugh, then rode on to the fences. They were in good shape, and I only paused a couple of times to hammer a strand of loose wire more firmly into the post. As we finished with the line, I wiped the sweat from my forehead and sighed.

"That's it," I said, sighing. "That wasn't much of a job at all."

"You didn't have any posts to mend," he said. "I did a bit of fence mending when I was a boy myself. Never did like fence."

"Why?" I asked.

"Well, Eric, it seems to me fences don't belong on the land. They close off people from people. They mark the land up like a map. This hill belongs to this man, this river belongs to that man. The rivers and the hills should belong to everybody."

"Then the cattle and the sheep and all the other animals would run all over everything," I said. "You'd get your corn crop and your garden trampled. You got to have fences."

"Only farmers need fences," he said. "There's

117

some men who've got to have everything planted in neat little rows. They got to fence everything, got to build houses and barns and cities. A man don't really need all that. The land can give life just the way it is. There's fish in the rivers and deer in the hills. There used to be buffalo all along the banks of the Cimarron.

"I've known men who never owned a single thing. They never put their feet in the same valley two years in a row. But you should've seen them, son. You never seen a man so full of life."

"I thought about living like that once," I said. "Like the Indians. Some of them used to ride by to the south. But I guess I wouldn't like to live that way much. The freedom would be great, but I'd miss having a home."

Fletcher didn't say anything else. He urged his horse onward, and I led the way to the creek. When we arrived, Tom and Willie were busy fishing. Willie ran over to us, screaming something and waving his hands in the air.

"I caught the biggest catfish you ever saw, Eric," Willie called out. "It's bigger than my whole leg."

I climbed down from my horse and lifted him into the air.

"Willie, you're a regular fisherman," I said, feeling him clamp down on my shoulder with his strong little hands. "Why don't you dip that pole of yours back into the creek and snag a couple more."

"Sure, Eric," he said, racing back to the creek.

"I'm sorry about all that, Mr. Fletcher," I said. "Willie's not too big, and he gets excited."

"Nothing to explain, son," Fletcher said.

"Did you go fishing when you were little?" I asked him.

"From time to time," he said. "We didn't live far from the river, and sometimes my brothers and I would finish our chores and run down there. We used to swim and fish and raise a little ruckus."

"I thought your brothers all died when they were little," I said.

"The war killed them all," he said, frowning. "The war took everything that had been and destroyed it."

"Mama never talked like that," I said. "She grew up in Texas, too."

"She never fought in the war," Fletcher said.

"I guess that's it," I said, matching his sadness.

We walked together out to the creek and joined Tom and Willie. We watched them fish awhile. Then Willie caught a sixth catfish, and we gathered around him.

"That's enough for supper," I said.

"Can we go swimming, Eric?" Willie asked, taking off his sweaty shirt.

"Sure," I said, smiling and pushing Tom in the water.

In a matter of minutes Willie and I were splashing into the creek, too. The water was cool, and I let myself sink into the muddy bottom.

Fletcher sat on a rock and watched us. There was a distant look in his eyes as if he was looking at us but remembering something else. He was with us, but he was also far away, lost in some other place and time. When we finally splashed out of the water, his eyes brightened, and he laughed at us.

"Never did see three boys splash so much water," he said. "Surprised you left any water in the creek."

We laughed with him, then scrambled into our

clothes.

"Reminds me of running through the river as a boy," Fletcher said to us. "I'd almost forgotten."

"Tell us about it," Tom begged.

"It's been a long time," Fletcher said. "A very long time."

"Tell us," we all said.

"Well, I wasn't much older than Eric at the time," he began as we sat down around his feet. "I rode with the son of the great Comanche chief, Yellow Shirt. Yellow Shirt had once killed seven enemies in battle in a single day. I hunted with his son. One morning I shot a bull buffalo that nearly killed the chief's son."

"Did they make you a member of the tribe?" I asked.

"You been listening to too many stories," Fletcher said, laughing. "I lived and hunted with the Comanches, but they never forgot I was a white man. I was never admitted to their sacred ceremonies, their councils. I was only a boy they took to their hearts."

"But the chief's son was your friend," I said. "You saved his life."

"But there was always a difference between us, son," Fletcher explained. "He was ready to die for his people, for his lands."

"You went to war for yours," I said.

"That's not why I went, Eric," he said. "I went to fight because I thought it would be a great adventure. I went because my father went. The life of a Comanche is simple, though. He eats, hunts, sleeps. His life never belongs to himself. When the time comes for him to die, he never even flinches."

"He dies for his people, just like Papa died for us," Willie said.

"Would you die for anyone, Mr. Fletcher?" I asked.

"No," he said. "I've never known anything or anyone I'd die for."

"Not even for your brothers?" I asked. "I mean if they'd lived."

"No," he said. "Life's hard enough on a man. I just try to get by as best I can. Tell me about your father."

"He was a good man," Tom said sadly.

"He was good with his hands," I said. "He was about the best carpenter you ever saw. We built the feed store all by ourselves. He came here with Mama and Tom and me, and he made us a home. I guess he was like the Comanches. He died for his people and his home."

"You'd be a good deal better off if he'd gone on living," Fletcher said.

"I don't know," I said. "Sometimes I think that, but I guess you have to make a stand sometimes. Being afraid all the time's no good."

"You have to make yourself strong enough that nobody can hurt you," Fletcher said.

"I'll be that strong someday," I said.

"Well, this is a good day to start," Fletcher said, standing up. "Come along, Eric."

"Yes, sir," I said, following him. "Willie, Tom, you take home the fish and help Mama, hear?"

"Sure," Tom said. "We'll see you at supper."

"Count on that," I said.

Fletcher got on his horse, and I climbed into my saddle, too. Then we rode back out to the fence line.

"You take out that Colt revolver and hand it to me," he said, sliding out of his saddle and down to the ground.

121

"What Colt revolver?" I asked, squirming.

"The one you put in your saddlebag as we were leaving," he told me.

"Yes, sir," I said, handing him the gun.

He opened the cylinder and examined it. He took the bullets out, then handed the gun back to me.

"This piece's clean," he said. "You keep it that way. A clean gun won't misfire. That can save your life."

"Yes, sir," I said.

"Now show me how you hold it."

I took the pistol in my right hand and held it with my fingers clutching it tightly.

"Loosen your grip, son, and hold it with both hands," he said.

"But I never saw a gunfighter hold a gun with two hands," I objected.

"Seen a lot of twelve-year-old gunfighters, have you?" he asked. "The first rule about shooting a gun is to have control. You're not going to control that Colt with one hand."

"Yes, sir," I said.

"Now squeeze the trigger a few times," he told me. "Get to be comfortable. When you get to where the gun feels like it's part of you, let me know."

I felt the gun, moved it around, pulled the trigger a few times and listened to the click of the hammer. My hands got used to the weight.

"Ready to try your aim?" he asked.

"Yes, sir," I said, handing him the gun.

Fletcher smiled as he loaded the gun. Then he set up some rocks on the fence posts and handed me the pistol.

"I want you to aim and fire at each rock," he

said. "Just take your time, son. It doesn't matter how fast you draw or fire if you don't hit what you aim for."

"Guess that's true," I said.

I raised the revolver and pointed it at the first rock. Then I took a deep breath and fired. The recoil of the gun stunned me a minute, and the bullet missed its mark.

"I missed," I said, looking at my feet.

"Happens," he told me. "Try again."

I shot off twenty bullets or so before I finally hit the rock. After that I began to improve. My shots hit the rocks more and more, and I got to where I was hitting one out of every two.

"Before I leave, you'll be able to hit five out of six," he told me. "You be sure to clean that gun now."

"I will sir," I said.

As we rode back to the house, we passed by the little graveyard on the hill. I stopped and walked over to Papa's grave. I stood there and said a little prayer for him. Then I walked back to my horse.

"How do the Comanches bury their dead people?" I asked. "I heard once they put them in caves."

"No, they bury them on platforms on a mountain. The spirit mountain, they call it. When the chief is ready to die, he climbs the mountain and prays. Then he dies. A warrior who's killed in battle is taken there."

"By his family?" I asked.

"Most of the time," he said. "And by his friends."

"I'd want to be buried here," I said. "I'd want my mother and my brothers here around my grave. I'd want to feel like I belonged. Papa and

Michael and even little Elsa would be at my side. I guess I'd feel warm knowing I was with them, that my sons, if I have any, will be here, too."

"There's times when a family comes in handy," he said, getting that faraway look in his eyes again.

"You can be part of our family, Mr. Fletcher," I said to him with a serious look in my eyes. "We could call you our uncle."

"You've got real uncles," he told me, looking away from me. "You don't need me."

He rode past me and made his way back to the house. As he rode, I told myself we really didn't need him. But in my heart I felt that maybe he needed us. I didn't really understand why I felt that way, but I was sure I was right.

XIV

That night as the sun went down, Tom, Willie and I cleaned up the kitchen and washed the dishes. Mama followed Fletcher outside, and the two of them sat down together on the porch. When the dishes were clean, I made my way over to the front window and listened to them talking. Mama would have skinned me alive if she'd known, but I wanted to know what was going on. There was something Fletcher was keeping secret, something about Mama, something about us. I just had to know what it was.

For a long time neither of them said anything. Then Mama took out a little envelope and read it to herself.

"Bad news?" Fletcher asked.

"It's from my brother back in Texas," she said. "He's offering to take us in, me and the boys. He says there's plenty of work on the ranch for growing boys. He says Sam Delamer never turned his back on his relations in all of his life."

"Then you're going?" Fletcher asked.

"I don't see what else we can do," Mama said sadly. "I thought about taking in sewing to help out, but Eric could never manage the crops."

"I wouldn't count that boy short. He's got spunk."

"I know," she said. "He's so small to be a man, though. At his uncle's place, he could grow up slowly. He'd have somebody to lean on."

"He's your boy, ma'am, but I'd say the day's past for him to lean on anybody. Once a boy steps out like a man, he's done it. There's no turning back."

"I know," Mama said. "The worst part of it is that he's got this hatred bottled up inside himself. You never knew my husband, but he was a man who believed in things. He was a lot like my brother Sam. They believed you fought for your home, died for your family. Eric remembers that. It's going to be hard to pull him away from this land."

"Have you talked it over with him?" Fletcher asked.

"I don't have to," she said. "He'll want to stay. No, the only way is to just up and do it. He'll resent it for some time, but once he gets to Texas, he'll forget all about it."

"Have you ever forgotten your home, ma'am?" he asked. "I mean the place you were born."

Mama paused a minute. Her face became wrinkled, and she frowned.

"No, I guess I haven't," she said. "I guess you never do."

"Then you have your answer," he said. "That boy's not going to be happy in Texas. He won't forget you ran away. I must've talked to him a hundred times about it. I told him sticking around a place waiting to get shot's a fool's play. That boy's got roots to him, though. He's a sticker."

"And you, Mr. Fletcher?" Mama asked. "What are you?"

"Not sure, ma'am," he said. "Once I thought I knew who I was. I was wrong, though. One thing I

126

know for sure. I was never a sticker. I never claimed to put my brand on the land. I never took to raising corn or milking cows.

"Guess you'd call me a roamer. I go here and there, never staying so long as to wear out my welcome. It's a different kind of life."

"Ever been married?" Mama asked.

"No," he said, laughing. "There've been ladies, sure, but nobody I ever found who could fence me in."

"You must be very lonely," Mama said. "Since John was killed, it seems the nights are never warm anymore. But at least I have the children."

"There's some comfort in that," Fletcher said. "Sometimes the loneliness seems to eat through me, but you see, I'm used to being by myself. I never really took to needing people, and most of 'em are pretty poor excuses for human beings anyway."

"You'll never convince me of that," she said. "You know, I've been watching you with the boys. Eric looks up to you like nobody I've ever seen. He loved his father, worked at his side since he was nine. But you he looks up at you like some sort of hero."

"That's the boy in him," Fletcher said. "I been followed around by little boys from Abilene to Cheyenne."

"Not by anyone like Eric," she said. "You've talked to him. He's not like most boys. He's got a quietness, a serious streak to him. He chooses his friends and his heroes very carefully, and he's loyal to them."

"Must take after his father," Fletcher said.

"No, he's not at all like John," Mama said. "Eric doesn't have the laughter. And Eric isn't content with getting by like John was. If John had lived long enough to leave Eric the farm, Eric would have built it into an empire. No, Eric reaches for things, wants things, dreams about being more than he is.

"He's like my second brother," Mama said, frowning. "We named Willie after him. My brother Willie was always the wild one. He'd go off on his own for weeks when he was just a little boy. Sam dreamed of building the ranch, but Willie dreamed of being a king or a general."

"What happened to him?" Fletcher asked.

"He died," Mama said, looking away from him. "It was the war. I got letters from him. In the beginning the letters spoke of heroes and grand balls and shiny brass buttons. But they grew sour. The war took away Willie's heart. In a way I'm glad he didn't live to be old. He's the kind who should always be a boy."

"How'd he die?" Fletcher asked.

"I don't know exactly," Mama said. "I got a letter from a friend of his. The letter just said that Willie was dead. There was some money with the letter. I set it aside so that maybe one of my boys could use it to go to school."

"Is your Willie like your brother then?" he asked.

"No," she said. "Michael was like Willie. Michael ran and played and laughed all day. Willie's more like Tom. They're steady like John was."

"How much would it take to get you through the next few years?" Fletcher asked. "I mean taking into account you stayed here and Eric got the garden and some crops in."

"I don't know," she said. "Maybe a few hundred dollars."

"If you had the feed store, could you run it?"

"There's not much to that," she said. "It's not far to town. Eric and Tom could help after school let out. Willie could even do some of the work."

"It would clear you a good profit, wouldn't you say?" he asked.

"Probably," she said.

"Then I've got a proposition for you, Mrs. Sheidler," he said. "I'd like to buy a corner of that feed store."

"That would hardly be a good bargain for you," Mama said. "Dunstan has a man in there. I don't really own it."

"Dunstan's man will be gone tomorrow night," he said. "I can promise you that. Now, what would you say to thirty dollars a month?"

"For only a corner of the store?" she asked. "What would you want it for?"

"I thought I might set up a little gunsmith shop."

"You're a gunsmith?" Mama asked.

"Yes," he told her. "It's a trade I learned in the army. As you may have suspected, I've had a good deal of experience with guns."

"You'd just be asking for trouble, Mr. Fletcher," Mama said. "That would be an open invitation to Dunstan to have you killed."

"That's what Dunstan intended the other night when he sent his men out here," he said. "Look, Mrs. Sheidler, all this is is a chance to get your store back, to stir up the people in town. Dunstan's on the run right now. If we take back the feed store, maybe the people in town will try to get back the bank, the other places, too."

"You've seen the people in town, Mr. Fletcher. They ride out here and look in on me nearly every day. It's not out of courtesy. It's because they want to know when you're going after Dunstan."

"Good," Fletcher said, his eyes suddenly darkening so that a chill ran down my backbone. "If the people think that way, so will Dunstan."

Mama stared at Fletcher. There was something strange in her eyes, too, a look of almost remembrance. It was as if she was close to knowing him, but the recollection was snatched away by the years that had separated the people they had been.

"This doesn't seem at all like you, Mr. Fletcher," she said. "You're suddenly making a stand here, for us. You've said a hundred times how no one or no place is ever worth making that stand. Why here and now? Why for us?"

"Ma'am, there's a reason," he said. "Maybe I remember a long time ago when I wasn't as free as I am now. Maybe you remind me of someone I used to know. Maybe I look into the faces of those boys and see the sons I've never had. I don't know.

"I do know there's something important about the way Eric talks. I can't help feeling like I was sent here for some strange reason. Maybe it's like a story I once heard an old Kiowa say."

"An Indian?" Mama asked.

"Yes, ma'am," Fletcher said. "He said there was once an Indian who used to hunt the buffalo and the deer, fish the great rivers, ride across a thousand sunsets. They say this man was a great warrior, but he never took anyone to his lodge. It seemed like his whole life was spent searching for a brave death.

"Then one morning he watched the sunrise, and he knew that was to be the day. Sure enough a hundred Pawnees rode against his village, and he led his men out to battle. He killed his enemies one by one. Then when the battle was won, a single Pawnee arrow flew through the air and struck him in the heart."

"And you think this is your last battle?" Mama asked.

"I don't know, ma'am," Fletcher told her. "I only know for the first time I can remember it seems more important to stay than go on."

"In that case, I'm glad," she said, taking his hand

and giving it a squeeze. "It's good to have a man around. It's hard for Eric to grow up with no one around to show the way. I hope you'll be around awhile."

"Yes, ma'am," he said. "I hope so, too, but I figure I'll be seeing that Kiowa's sunrise any time now."

The air was filled with silence for a long time. I could tell they were thinking about what they'd said, and I walked away. I got out the pistol and slipped out the back door to the barn. Then I began cleaning the gun.

When I was nearly finished with the job, I heard footsteps near the door. I slid behind a table and watched to see who it was. For a minute I was paralyzed with fear. I thought Dunstan's men had returned. Then I saw that it was Fletcher.

"Where are you, boy?" he asked quietly. "I saw you come out here to clean your gun."

"Here I am, sir," I said, standing up.

"You do a good job?" he asked.

"Yes, sir," I said. "I haven't fired it too many times, but I've been cleaning it most of my life."

I handed him the gun and watched him inspect it. He checked the barrel, the cylinder, the firing pin, even the trigger. When he finished, he handed me back the pistol and sat down, a smile crossing his face.

"How would you like to run a feed store?" he asked.

"I've done it," I said. "Papa used to leave me in charge while he worked the fields. I'm good with figures, and I've got a strong back when it comes to moving sacks of grain or seed."

"Tomorrow we're riding into town," he told me. "You're going to open the feed store. Afraid?"

131

I felt a shiver work its way through me.

"Yes, sir," I told him.

"Good, you're being honest with me," he said. "You can handle it, can't you?"

"Yes, sir," I said, smiling. "Papa'd be happy knowing we're going to get the store back."

"All right," Fletcher said. "Tomorrow bright and early we ride in. You carry that pistol in your belt. All the time, son. You know Dunstan's men. You see one of them, pull it out and tell him to leave. If he draws, you put a hole in him. Don't flinch, son, just shoot. You hesitate and we'll be putting up another white cross on that hill of yours."

"I won't freeze," I said, glaring at him with eyes full of hatred for the men who'd killed my father.

"Sleep good tonight," he said. "We're doing what they call in the army forcing the issue. We're making Dunstan make his best move. He's got to show his hand."

"Figure we can take him?" I asked.

"You'd better, too," he told me. "Better forget all the softness you've known. Forget about your ma and brothers. You just think about how that man gunned down your pa right in front of you. You remember the blood, the cold you felt inside your stomach. Then you can kill anybody real easy."

I felt my insides twist into a knot as he spoke. That night when I finally fell asleep, I saw Papa over and over again. I saw the emptiness that filled his eyes as he lay on the floor of the feed store. A fierce rage burned through me, and there was no room left for fear, only hatred.

XV

We rode into town early that next morning. There was still a yellow glow hanging over the horizon, and the morning mist clung to the land like an old woman's shawl. As we passed the little cantina and proceeded on up Front Street, I looked at Fletcher's face.

There was a grim smile on his lips, and his eyes were colder than even the day he'd shot down Tripp Hunt. The rim of his cavalry hat cast a shadow over his forehead, and his back was stiff as a board. He looked like some kind of avenging angel on his way to strike down the devil himself.

Only a few people were out on the street so early in the morning, and they didn't seem to notice us. Only Mr. Cooper, the barber, looked up and waved to me. I frowned and looked away the same way Fletcher did.

We arrived at the feed store a few minutes later. I took out my key and opened the front door. Then we walked inside.

"Dunstan never got a reputation for keeping a place clean," Fletcher said to me as he brushed a layer of dust from one of the shelves. "Looks like the whole store could use a cleaning."

"I'll get the broom," I said. "It doesn't take too long to sweep up."

"First things first," Fletcher told me. "Seems to me there's something uglier on that front window. You think you can clean it off?"

I stared at him for a minute, not understanding what he was talking about. Then I noticed the cloth with Dunstan's name on it that had been nailed over our name.

"Right away," I said, taking a hammer and racing out front to clear away the cloth. I tore off the cloth, then pried off the plank over the door. I returned in triumph.

"Hold onto that," Fletcher told me. "You might need some fuel for the fire this winter."

"Yeah," I said, laughing.

We next started restocking the shelves. Dunstan's men had reordered seed and grain, but they hadn't put anything where it belonged. My arms ached under the load of the heavy sacks, but I managed to get most of them in their correct places before noon.

Fletcher busied himself with setting up a small table in the corner of the store. He had some tools for repairing guns, a few screws and pins and such. I noticed, though, that he never took his eyes off the door.

After the shelves were restocked, I started sweeping the floor. Then we waited for our first customer to arrive. No one came until well past noon, though. I guess the people expected we'd be gone by then, and they didn't want Dunstan coming around to demand payment for something they'd already paid us for.

The first to come inside was Mr. Roderick. He strode through the door with a huge smile on his face. Then he ran over to me and lifted me right off the ground.

"Eric, my boy, it does a man's heart good to see you," the huge man told me. "This town hasn't been the same without you running up Front Street, throwing rocks at the horses, laughing at Jimmy Kinsey's fool jokes."

"It's good to see you, too, sir," I said. "You remember Mr. Fletcher."

Mr. Roderick glanced over at Fletcher.

"How are you, sir?" Mr. Roderick asked.

"Fair," Fletcher said, never taking his eye from the door.

"What is it I can do for you, Mr. Roderick?" I asked. "Some grain or oats maybe?"

"I can always use oats," the man told me. "I haven't been buying from Dunstan. I figure I can use maybe seven, eight sacks. You still have any of that good horse liniment your papa used to keep around?"

"Yes, sir," I said.

"Three bottles of that, too. Boy, it's a pure delight to see you back o' that counter," Mr. Roderick said, smiling all over. "Does a man's heart good, purely does."

I got the liniment and started pulling the sacks of oats off the shelves.

"You let me tend to them sacks," Mr. Roderick said. "Wouldn't do to have you straining yourself. Here," he said, lifting the sack like a baby lifting a rattle. "You figure the bill."

"Yes, sir," I said.

By the time he'd carried the sacks down the street to the stable, four or five other customers had come in. Papa always gave credit, and I tallied their accounts.

"I think it might be best if we took the money to

135

your mother," Mr. Gunther told me. "Dunstan might try to worm it out of you here."

"Yes, sir," I said, nodding to the man. Mr. Gunther had the farm just the other side of the railroad, and he and Papa had played cards together on Saturday night for five years.

"You surely are looking more like your papa every day," Mr. Gunther told me, squeezing my shoulder with his rough hand. "I miss him, son."

"We all do," I said, frowning.

When the last customer left, the store was left to the silence of my own thoughts. Then I heard the sound of heavy footsteps on the porch, and Fletcher tensed up. John Hazlett, a young man who'd come to town a few years earlier, walked through the door. John had been a runner over at the telegraph office awhile. Then he'd worked as a clerk over at the hotel. Lately he'd been working for Dunstan.

"Didn't know Dunstan had taken you onto his payroll, Eric," he said to me.

I stared hard into his bright blue eyes. There had been a time when we'd been friends. We'd gone fishing some, and Papa had taken John into our house when the young man had broken his leg once.

"What do you want?" I asked.

"Nothing much," John told me. "I just heard the feed store was doing some fine business this morning, and I thought I'd best check it out. You see, I heard Carl Morgan had left town, and I didn't remember Mr. Dunstan giving anybody else the job."

"Dunstan doesn't own this place," I said. "He stole it from my father."

"Stole might be a hard word for it," John said. "Some might say he collected it off your father for a debt."

"There are always a few liars," I said, biting my lip

136

to keep from losing my temper.

"This your cash box?" John asked, putting his hand on the metal box. "I might check the receipts."

"You might get your fool head blown off, too," Fletcher said, walking over. "A man can find all sorts of ways to get himself killed if he halfway tries. You don't seem old enough to want to get yourself buried, son."

"You might be surprised who'd get buried," John said, knocking my hand away from the cash box.

Fletcher reached out and knocked John to the ground. Fletcher had moved like lightning. I'd never seen a man do anything so fast. John sat on the floor for several minutes, totally stunned. Then he wiped away a trickle of blood from his mouth and stood up.

"You're a dead man, mister," John said, shaking with rage. "You can count the day left of your life on one hand."

"I'd call that big talk," Fletcher said, laughing. "Boy, you'd best keep your hands to yourself you want to get any older."

"You don't understand, do you?" John asked. "I'm going to kill you. And then I'm going to take that pretty rebel hat of yours and throw it to the pigs."

"You'd better leave," I said to John. "You'd better get out of town."

"No, you'd better leave," John said, pointing his long skinny finger at me. "You'd better run to that uncle of yours, the one with the big ranch. You'd better find a place to hide because when Dunstan gets finished, there won't be enough left of you to bury."

"That's about enough," Fletcher said, stepping back and dangling his hand at his side. "You got something you want to do, do it!"

John froze. There was something terribly deadly about Fletcher just then. The whole room filled with a chill, and I figured someone was about to die.

"You're awful lucky, mister," John finally said. "I've got a feeling for this boy. His pa put me up when I broke my leg. Otherwise you'd be dead and buried this day. I'd have killed you by now except I wouldn't have Eric here see you die. Do yourself a favor. Get out of town. Leave Mr. Dunstan to tend to his own affairs. You keep sticking your nose in where it don't belong, you may lose it altogether."

"You finished?" Fletcher asked.

John just stared at him.

"Now let me tell you something," Fletcher said. "I could just as easily've killed you a few minutes ago. My hand wouldn't have taken any longer to fire my pistol than to slap you down. You're young, son, maybe even a little fast. But you'd be just as dead, just as cold as if you were slow. You tell him there's been enough death."

"You'd best remember what I said," John said. "Leave town while you can. You, too, Eric. I liked your pa. I'd hate for him to have no son left to carry on his name."

Before Fletcher could say anything, John slipped out the door and disappeared. After that no one came to the store that day.

It must have been about an hour before supper when Jake Steele walked into our midst. I was about ready to close up, and I barely heard him come inside. Fletcher heard, though, and the two men stood across the store from each other.

"Your name Fletcher?" Steele asked.

"That's right," Fletcher said. "There's those who call me that."

"Mr. Dunstan wants to see you," Steele said.

138

"If he wants to see Mr. Fletcher, tell him he can just come over here and see him," I said, walking over to them. "Mr. Fletcher will wait for him."

"Little kids that get into Mr. Dunstan's business don't get to grow bigger," Steele said with a tone that chilled me through to the bone.

"You tell Dunstan I'll be down to see him," Fletcher said calmly. "You tell him something else, too. You tell him a flea bites this boy or his family 'cause Dunstan put 'em up to it, I'll be around to see it's paid for. You tell him a board's touched at this store, his hide won't be worth a plug nickel."

"You tell him yourself," Steele said, laughing. "Mr. Dunstan's got big plans for you. For all of you," he said, looking at me. "He says he knows Apaches who like to buy small white boys down in New Mexico. I believe they eats 'em."

Fletcher swung his hand over beside his gun, and Steele backed away.

"It's not my play, Fletcher," Steele said, "I'll be killing you, that's for sure, but not before you talk to Mr. Dunstan. He's got words for you."

"You tell Dunstan he'd best start saying his prayers," Fletcher said. "You tell your buddies over at the saloon that any of them in town after tomorrow are dead men. I plan to start trimming the tree so to speak."

"You talk mighty tough, mister," Steele said, laughing. "We've got five or six guns over there."

"You had twenty last week," I said, shaking out of my terror.

Steele's face turned a sickly shade of yellow. Then he walked outside, slamming the door behind him.

"You're not really going?" I asked Fletcher. "Tell me you were just saying that."

"It's got to be done, Eric," Fletcher said. "Now

139

let's shut this place up and get some supper. I'm starving."

"Yes, sir," I said.

We rode out of town together. This time Front Street was lined with people. I felt their heavy gaze on my shoulders, and I knew they figured we'd come back to town that night and kill Dunstan.

I couldn't help wondering as I looked into their faces why they didn't get out their rifles and go over there themselves. All they had to do was wipe out six men, but I guess killing is a hard thing to do when you haven't got a heart full of hate. And facing death is harder still.

Somehow I didn't feel like I was afraid of getting shot. Fletcher was cool as ice, and he was more than a match for them. If I got shot, it didn't matter as long as Dunstan didn't survive, as long as Mama and Tom and Willie could keep the farm.

But as we got close to home and I saw the house, I knew I was lying to myself. I loved being alive, riding through the fields, watching the sunsets and swimming in the creek. I was scared of dying, and I didn't want it to happen. I wished somebody else was the oldest. But somebody else wasn't. I was. And in all my life I'd never asked anybody else to do what I had to do.

XVI

We sat around the supper table that night staring at each other in silence. Mama and my brothers noticed the grim look in Fletcher's eyes, and they kept their thoughts to themselves. There really wasn't anything to be said. We'd all known the day would come when the man would ride into town and stand up to Dunstan. Now that time had come.

After supper, I followed Fletcher to the barn. He stood beside his horse, flexing the muscles in his leg.

"It still bothers you, doesn't it?" I asked. "You shouldn't go in there tonight, not when your leg's bothering you."

"Son, that's just an excuse. It's got to be done. You knew when you first spoke to me that you wanted me to face down Dunstan. Now why all the talk about it?"

"I didn't know you back then," I said. "I hate to say it, but I was just looking for somebody to shoot them all down. It's not that easy anymore.

Now I'm scared."

"It all goes back to what I told you before, Eric," he said, turning to me. "You get close to people, they end up hurting you. I know that's hard for you to understand just now, but it's the truth."

"Yes, sir," I said.

"You want to saddle my horse?" he asked.

"Sure," I said. "You want your rifle?"

"Won't need it," he said. "Just my handgun," he added, slapping his holster.

I lifted his cavalry saddle onto the horse and pulled the straps tight. Then I led the horse over and went back to saddle my own horse.

"Eric, you're not coming," he said, stopping me from taking my saddle.

"Sure I am," I said, facing him. "It has to be done with me, too. I've been practicing with my pistol. I can shoot pretty straight."

"That's not it," Fletcher said, putting a heavy hand on my shoulder. "There'll be no shooting tonight, son. This is just a little talk with Dunstan. Nothing too important."

"I'm not a little kid anymore," I said, pulling away from him.

"Look, Eric, life's going to be hard enough on you without hurrying it along. I'm not going to be here forever. As long as I am, why don't you let me handle this?"

"But you don't know Dunstan," I said, grabbing his hand. "He'll shoot you in the back. He won't give you a chance."

"Son, I know more than you do about this. This is my business, my work. I know all about what's going to happen. You'd best stay here."

I looked into his cold eyes and felt strangely calm. He didn't seem worried, didn't seem even concerned. I stepped away and watched him mount his horse. Then he rode past me into town.

I watched the moonlight dance across his broad shoulders. For a minute I just watched him. Then something inside me snapped, and I started walking after him.

The night seemed eerie. The moon was full and bright, and a million stars seemed to be peering down at me. There was something haunting about that moon, and I felt an urgent need to get to town.

It was only a mile to walk, but the going was always difficult at night. Sometimes rattlesnakes crossed the road, and there were always holes to step into that could snap a leg. I was used to darkness, though, and the moon was bright. I hurried along, afraid I'd miss something.

When I reached town, I looked at the lights shining out from the saloon. Music played on a piano rolled through the air, and I breathed easier. Nothing could have happened if the piano player was still playing.

I crept along the side of the street, hiding in the safety of the shadows. I hadn't forgotten the beating I'd gotten the last time I'd walked around town by myself. When I reached the side window of the saloon, I sat down and looked inside.

Fletcher was standing at the bar sipping on a tall mug of beer. His eyes glanced around the room, waiting for something to happen.

"Dunstan around?" Fletcher asked at last.

"Might be," the bartender said. "Who wants to know?"

"Me!" Fletcher said, slamming down the mug on the counter and looking at the bartender with cold eyes.

"Take it easy, mister," the bartender said. "I'll get him."

The bartender hurried off into Dunstan's office, and the men inside the saloon began walking out the door. Only John Hazlett and two others remained. The piano player finished his song and started to walk away.

"Stay and play awhile," Fletcher told the man.

"Please, mister," the piano player said, "I've got a wife and three kids."

"Go on," Fletcher said, and the man raced out the door and disappeared down the street.

Now silence filled the saloon, and I could see John and the other two men grow nervous. Fletcher just went on sipping his beer, paying no attention to anything else. Then Dunstan walked out of his office, and I fixed my eyes on him.

Dunstan hadn't been a young man for a long time. Streaks of gray were brushed through what had once been coal black hair, and his forehead was wrinkled. The man's nose was big, dominating the rest of his face. His teeth were yellow, and three of them were missing.

Dunstan wore a pair of tooled boots and black trousers. His shirt was also black. His silver revolver flashed in the light of a glass chandelier. He usually wore a wide-brimmed hat, but it was missing, revealing a receding hairline.

Dunstan walked over to the bar and glanced around. When Fletcher turned his way, Dunstan's face became white as a sheet.

"Hello, Kid," Dunstan said at last, leaning

144

against a barstool.

"Mike," Fletcher said, nodding.

In the silence that followed, a nervous shiver worked its way through my insides. They knew each other.

"Last heard you were out West," Dunstan said. "Up to Wyoming, then around Denver."

"Was," Fletcher said.

"It's been awhile since our days on the Cimarron, huh?" Dunstan asked.

"Awhile," Fletcher said.

"What's your play, Starr?" Dunstan asked, his forehead wrinkling up with concern.

"No play," Fletcher said.

"You weren't sent for?" Dunstan asked, seeming confused.

"No, just meeting the train," Fletcher said. "Figured to pass on through, maybe head down toward Santa Fe."

"And Hunt?"

"He pressed me. You know me, Mike, I don't like being pressed."

"You sure have broken up my plans. Especially when you got Corby Johnson. You couldn't've taken Johnson six years ago. He's the fastest I've ever seen."

"You haven't seen me lately. Six years is a long time, Mike."

"Meaning?"

"Meaning it might be best if you headed out of town."

"Out of town? Starr, I've put out a lot of money to get a grip on this town. There's a future here. We've got half the shops already. It isn't just anywhere you find the people willing to let you

145

walk all over them."

"Not everyone let you walk over them," Fletcher said, glaring at Dunstan.

"You mean Sheidler," Dunstan asked. "What's this kid mean to you, anyway?"

"What's anyone ever meant to me, Mike?" Fletcher asked. "Maybe he reminds me a little of myself. Maybe I'd like to see him get a little better shake than I ever had. Maybe enough Sheidlers have gotten killed."

"Listen, Starr," Dunstan said, sitting down beside him at the bar. "We can reach an understanding. The Sheidlers can keep the feed store. We won't bother them. You've got my word on that."

"Before you sent your boys out to the arn that would've been enough," Fletcher said. "Not now."

"I didn't know it was you, Starr," Dunstan said. "You've got to believe that."

"Why?"

"Because of what I was to you. Down on the Cimarron you were a snotty-nosed kid. You'd been up in Virginia shooting Yankees, but you didn't know nothing about killing men. You'd never've lasted a year out there without me."

"I'm what I am because of you, Mike," Fletcher said.

"Damn right you are. I looked after you. I made you top gun on the Cimarron. You made more gold in a month out there than any three men."

"I was only still young when I got to the Cimarron," Fletcher said. "Mike, you showed me everything you knew. But you didn't know life. You only knew death. You know I don't even know how many men I've killed. I've gotten to where it doesn't matter whether they're good or bad, friends or enemies. I just kill."

"Don't put that onto my back, Starr. A man can always walk away from it."

"No, he can't," Fletcher said angrily. "The moment I walked into town your man Hunt started after me. No, once you've taken the road we have, you're stuck with it."

"You owe me," Dunstan said. "I kept you alive."

"Maybe we'd both be better off if you hadn't, Mike. Anyway, I'll give you a week. After that I'll come for you. And if a single man rides out to the Sheidler place, if a single man comes to the feed store, if a single threat is made against any member of that family, you're dead."

"I'd never thought of it," Dunstan said, frowning. "Billy Starr shielding a bunch of farmers. Never thought I'd see the day."

"One week, Mike," Fletcher said, looking at Dunstan with a coldness that sent shivers down my spine.

Dunstan stood up and walked back to his office. Then Fletcher walked over and sat down at the table with John Hazlett and the other men.

"I just have a few words to say to you boys," Fletcher said. "Dying's a real easy thing to do. Men do it every day. It only takes the flash of a gun. The thing about dying is that once it's done, there's nothing else a man can do with his life. It's real important you do your dying for something important.

"Mike Dunstan in there has pouches of gold for his trouble. What've you got? Fifty dollars? That's not much to die for. I told Mike he's got himself a week. You boys have until tomorrow. Next time I see any of you, you'll be dead."

"Talk comes cheap," John Hazlett said, standing up.

"Not half as cheap as dying," Fletcher said, stepping back. "Seems like a shame somebody so young's in such a hurry to die."

"Try me," John said.

The other men stepped to one side. Then John drew his gun. Before the gun was out of its holster, Fletcher shot it from John's hand. Then Fletcher swung the pistol in John's direction and smiled cruelly.

"Now you got something else to say?" Fletcher asked.

"Please, mister," John said, his face pale as a ghost. "Please don't pull that trigger. I'm gone. I won't even ask Dunstan for my pay. I'm a ghost. You'll never see me again. I promise."

"What about you boys?" Fletcher asked, pointing the gun at the other men.

"We're gone," one of them said. "Tonight. This minute."

"Get!" Fletcher said, stomping his foot down. "Don't you ever come back here."

"Yes, sir," they said, racing out the door of the saloon and tumbling into the street.

As silence once again filled the saloon, Dunstan's door cracked open, and the man stepped into the saloon.

"Tough luck, Mike," Fletcher said. "Seems like you lost three more men."

Dunstan's face grew red, but his hand stayed clear of his holster.

"One week, Mike, that's all," Fletcher said.

Then Fletcher walked out the door and made his way to where I sat.

"I thought you were staying home," he said to me.

"Are you really Billy Starr?" I asked. "I've heard of you."

"Was once," he said. "You were supposed to stay at the farm."

"I couldn't," I told him. "I belonged here."

"Well, come on," he said. "Climb up behind me on the saddle. It's a short ride back."

I smiled as I climbed up behind him on his horse. He was a hard man, but I suddenly felt close to him. I didn't really understand why, but I leaned against him. As we rode on into the night, I felt we'd won our great battle.

XVII

The next five days flew by. Only two of Dunstan's men stayed in Whitlow. The others rode out with John Hazlett after Fletcher's meeting with Dunstan in the saloon. The bank and the mercantile reopened under their former managers, and the people in town seemed to sense the difference.

Only the saloon remained in Dunstan's hands. It was closed most of the time, and nobody except Dunstan and his men entered. Even the piano player and bartender vanished. Fletcher spent most of his time working on guns at his table in the feed store. I kept the business going, and nearly every farmer in the valley came by at one time or another.

Fletcher and I were on our way down to the little Mexican cantina when we heard the doors of the saloon swing open. A tall man dressed completely in black stepped out onto the street and glared at us.

He was a man unlike others. His black shirt had two rows of pearl buttons, and his dark brown hair was combed back away from his forehead. There was a look of youth to him, but his eyes were old, deadly like a rattlesnake. He had a wicked smile, and he laughed in a devilish manner.

"Howdy there," the man called out. "I believe you're the man I'm looking for."

Fletcher turned toward him and pushed me away.

"They call me Deacon," the man in black went on to say. "Harry Deacon."

"I heard of you," Fletcher said, spitting on the ground.

"They say you're Billy Starr," Deacon said.

"Some called me that," Fletcher said.

"You been causing Mr. Dunstan considerable inconvenience," Deacon said. "He asked me to persuade you to tend to your own business."

"That right?" Fletcher asked. "Seems like to me it's you who might tend his own business."

"Mr. Dunstan's made it my business," Deacon said. "He says you're good enough to be worth two thousand dollars. That so?"

"I guess you'll never know," Fletcher said. "If you take Dunstan's money, you'll never have a chance to spend it."

"That right?" Deacon said, laughing. "Starr? I could take you on the worst day of my life."

"When?" Fletcher asked, his eyes blazing.

"Noon tomorrow," Deacon said. "Right here."

"Make your peace tonight," Fletcher said. "You'll be dead this time tomorrow."

"Or you will," Deacon said, smiling cruelly.

I fixed my eyes on the man dressed in black. I felt my knees shaking. Then I felt Fletcher's hand on my shoulder.

"You hungry?" he asked.

"Not anymore," I said.

"How about let's close the store and ride back to the farm. I feel like an afternoon of fishing."

"You haven't been fishing since you got here," I said, looking into his eyes. "You worried?"

151

"Aren't you?" he asked. "You should be. Deacon changes everything."

We rode back to the farm without saying anything. I caught the looks of fear in the eyes of the townspeople. They'd seen Deacon, too.

Back at the farm we rode out to the creek and sat down on the bank.

"Tell me about him," I said.

"Deacon?" he asked.

"Yes, sir," I said. "You know him?"

"I heard of him. He gunned down a sheriff in Taos last year. Killed three men in a gunfight down Santa Fe way. He's quick as a rattler and twice as deadly. He never shot a man he wasn't paid to kill."

"Can you handle him?" I asked.

"I never saw him draw, son," Fletcher said. "It's always a question of the little things when you face a top gun. It's how shaky a morning you had, how much hate you've got, how much you've got to lose if you get yourself shot."

"It'll be all right," I said.

"Always has been," he said to me.

"Was it like this your first time?" I asked.

"That was a long time ago," he said, leaning back against the trunk of an oak tree. "It was down on the Cimarron."

"That's where they called you Starr?"

"That was later," he said. "I was in a little town back then. I'd just left the war, still had what was left of my uniform on. I was a full major in the Texas cavalry. Some man goaded me into a fight. I didn't have much time to think. He was a little drunk, and I was scared to death. I pulled out my cavalry pistol and blew the top of his head off."

"What then?" I asked.

"I went over and threw up. A little later Mike

152

Dunstan found me."

"What did he do?"

"Well, he wasn't such an old man then. He was about the fastest around. He took me under his wing, taught me to draw. We were fighting for the McNallys in the range war. At first I just rode along. I thought we were fighting for a kind of justice. It was like the war all over again. But the truth was that we were getting hired to kill men who were hired to kill us. After you shoot a few men, it doesn't much matter why you do it anymore."

"If you had it all to do over again, would you do the same thing?" I asked.

"Eric, I don't think any man ever starts out to be a killer. He gets into it by bits and pieces. I started out figuring I was shooting men that needed killing. But in truth I'm no one to judge. Just because I have quick hands shouldn't make it so I can decide whether a man should live or die.

"Anyway, what I'm trying to say, Eric, is that I haven't made my own way in this life. My life's made me. I never set out to be what I am. Son, it's awful important to watch out for yourself when you're young. You just have to lose a grip on your life for a little bit of time, and you never get it back."

"How could you stay with a man like Dunstan?" I asked.

"Wasn't easy," he said. "I rode to war with my father. He was a great man, a soldier, a patriot, a man who came to a land full of cactus and Indians and carved out an empire. The Yankees killed him, though, and I found myself alone.

"I was only sixteen when I first saw battle. It was bloody and ugly, and I knew it stained a man so that he could never go back to the peace of the valley he'd grown up in."

"You said you were a major in the army," I said.

"At nineteen," he told me. "I was good at soldiering. After my father died, I just didn't care anymore. They all thought it was courage. They have ever since. It's really that death doesn't scare me. That's how it gets when life is hard and ugly all the time."

"It seems like we always talk about killing and dying," I said.

"It's not what I brought you out here to talk about," he said.

"Then what?" I asked.

"Something I know now I can't say to you, Eric. It's something you'll find out one day from somebody else."

"You can tell me anything," I said. "I can take it."

"That's not the problem," he said. "It's me. I thought I'd find something inside myself, but it's not there. You can't close yourself off from people for ten years, then suddenly find your feelings again."

He walked away for a minute, and I stared into the water. Then he returned, looking into my eyes with a sadness different from any I'd seen before.

"We'd better head back to the house," he said. "Your mother will start worrying."

"Yes," I said, following him to the horses.

As we rode along, I kept looking into his eyes. I kept thinking to myself that those eyes were hiding something.

"When it's all over tomorrow, I mean if you get out of it all right, are you staying?" I finally asked.

"Thought some about it," he said.

"We could use you," I said. "I wish you would. Mama likes you. I know she wants you to stay. Tom and Willie, too."

"And you?" he asked.

"You know how I feel," I said. "We need you.

154

Papa's gone, and there's nobody here to protect us. I try, Mr. Fletcher, but I'm not much of a man. I'm even little to be a boy. There's so much to learn, so much to do, and there's nobody around to show me how."

"Eric, you had a father," he said. "I could never be that to you, son. Tomorrow I'll go to town and kill a man. Maybe he'll kill me. Sooner or later a faster man always comes along. I'd leave or else be shot. That's not the man you're looking for to teach you about life."

"But if you could stay even a little while, a year or so."

"You don't need me, son. You already know more about living than a lot of people. You'll grow to be the kind of man I would've liked to be."

"You're sure you won't stay?"

"Some things just can't be, Eric."

I stayed up late that night. It was stormy outside, and the thunder sounded like the gunshots I knew would come in the morning. I walked over to the window and sat down on the floor. Then I looked out at the puddles that were forming in the barnyard.

"You awake, Eric?" Tom asked, sitting up in bed. "You all right?"

"Sure," I said. "What could be wrong?"

"Something sure is," Tom said. "You didn't eat your supper, and you've been walking around with your head down all night. It's like when Papa died."

"Yeah," I said, "that's just what it's like."

"He's going away, isn't he?" Tom asked.

"Tomorrow," I said. "Dunstan sent for a fast gun, a killer from Santa Fe. I figure maybe this new man, Deacon, might be faster than Mr. Fletcher."

"And Mr. Fletcher's going to go away?" Tom asked.

"Mr. Fletcher's going to fight this Deacon," I told him. "And Dunstan's got a couple of other men. I think maybe Mr. Fletcher's going to get himself killed."

"I like Mr. Fletcher, Eric," Tom said. "I don't know him too good, but he's a nice man. He never yells at you when you bother him, and he showed Willie and me how to make all kinds of things with leather."

"I wish he'd stay," I said.

"Let's ask him, Eric," Tom said. "I'll bet he would."

"No," I said. "I already asked him."

"Maybe if Mama baked a pie," Tom said. "Nobody ever passed up one of Mama's pies."

"It's not that," I said. "I think he's gotten to like us. I think maybe he's fighting this man just for us. There's something sad about Mr. Fletcher. I don't think he cares whether he lives or dies."

"I know," Tom said. "It used to scare me, but then I got to know him some. It's like he wants to be nice, but he's scared to."

"He's afraid to let people care about him," I said. "I hope I never get to be that way, Tom. I'd hate to die knowing nobody would cry over me."

"Mama would," Tom said. "Willie, too."

"Yeah," I said.

"I would, too," Tom said. "I know I'd be the man of the family then, but I'd still cry, just like I did when Michael and Papa died. It's all right, isn't it?"

"I guess so," I said. "Even if it isn't, there's not much you can do about it. I cried when Papa got shot, and I was twelve already."

"Yeah, and I'm only eleven," Tom said.

"You suppose when this is all over Mama will let us stay here?" I asked. "You suppose she'll forget about going to Texas?"

156

"She already has," Tom said. "I saw her write a telegram to Uncle Sam. She said some things I don't understand, but she mainly said this is our home, and we're going to fight for it. That's what Papa would have done."

"Yeah," I said. "I wish I knew what's the best thing to do. Papa always knew just what to do."

"Mr. Fletcher'll know," Tom said. "Ask him."

"I will," I said.

I then walked back to the bed and climbed in beside Tom. As I gave myself up to my weariness, I prayed Fletcher would be around tomorrow for me to ask.

XVIII

After breakfast that next morning Fletcher and I rode off to look over the fence line. At least that's what we told Mama. The real reason was so I could show off my shooting. Fletcher set up six rocks on the fence posts, then walked over to my side.

"When I say to fire, shoot at them," he told me. "Don't rush yourself, son. Just squeeze the rounds off one at a time. Ready?"

"Yes, sir," I said, fingering the holster nervously.

"Fire!" he yelled.

I pulled out the pistol and put both hands on the stock. Then I swung the barrel around and fired at each rock in turn. The blast was deafening, and the air was filled with powdersmoke. My eyes burned from it. As I lowered the gun, Fletcher slapped me on the back.

"Four of six," he said, laughing loudly. "Not bad for a kid."

"I'll be able to hit them all before long," I said. "And when I get bigger, I won't have to use both hands."

"You figure you'll be shooting the buttons off a man's coat, huh?"

"I'll get to be good like you," I said. "I'll get to be good enough people won't push me around."

"And the killing? Tell me, Eric, you figure you can kill a man?"

"If I have to," I said. "If I'd had a gun, I could have shot Hunt. I could kill a man to protect my family."

"That's always how it starts," Fletcher said, sighing. Then he walked back to the fence to set up the targets again.

"Starts?" I asked.

"There's no ending to it," he said. "Once you kill a man in a gunfight, you've made your choice. Then it's killing and more killing until you've killed yourself."

"Papa was killed, and he was no gunfighter," I said.

"Then learn to shoot, Eric. Learn to stay alive, but don't go out of your way to force something. Don't fight just anyone. Only when you find somebody you can't live with."

"That's how you started," I said. "Does it work?"

"Not for me," he said. "But maybe you can make it work, Eric. You've got something to hang onto. Maybe that'll make some kind of difference."

"How do you do it? The gunfighting, I mean. I know I'll have to wait until I'm bigger to really draw, but tell me about the other parts."

"By the time the draw comes, everything's decided," he said. "First you have to remember to keep your eyes on your target. No matter what he says or does, don't take your eyes off his hands."

"His hands?" I asked.

"A man doesn't shoot with his toes. I've seen men sit there and never move a muscle in their face. They just draw their piece and blast you. So you watch their hands. They can't shoot you with their mouths.

"Another thing. Get to know your piece. Try some different guns. Me, I use a long barrel for balance. Some use a light gun. I knew a man down on the Cimarron who had a handle carved to fit his hand. You pick a gun that feels natural. Then you keep it clean as a whistle. You keep it loaded with fresh bullets. Powder can go bad. A misfire can get you killed."

"You told me that," I said.

"I could tell you a hundred times, and it wouldn't be too often."

"What else is there?" I asked.

"The hardest thing of all," he said. "And the thing that keeps a top gun alive."

"What's that?" I asked.

"Knowing your man," he said. "Know everything there is to know about him. If he's got a weakness, find it. Use it against him. Even a little thing can keep you alive against a faster man."

"What about Deacon?" I asked. "What's his weakness?"

"Well, I never seen him draw, son, but I heard down in Santa Fe once that he thinks a bit too highly of himself. All those pearl buttons and all bear it out. But the thing that'll get him killed is that he blinks just before he draws. That breaks a man's concentration just enough."

"And you?"

"Talk down on the Cimarron was that I didn't have the heart to kill a man. They said I'd shoot for the shoulder or for the legs. They say I hold my gun too tight, I tense up. They say I froze when somebody talked about the war."

"But nobody shot you."

"Two of them did," he said. "Getting shot breaks a

160

man of bad habits. Now I shoot to kill. I don't draw on a man unless I'm ready to kill him."

"But you didn't shoot John Hazlett in the saloon last night," I reminded him.

"Well, I'm still not the sort to blast boys," he told me. "That boy wasn't fast enough to get himself killed. If his gun had cleared his holster, he'd be dead right now."

"You don't shoot for the arms or the legs anymore?"

"A man can still shoot you if he's wounded," Fletcher said. "A dead man can't shoot you. I don't generally face off against a man unless he needs killing. Good men don't go looking to die. And I'm as cold as stone on a winter's night in the Rockies now."

"Not all the time," I said. "You still care. I've been watching you. You sit down with Willie, and I can see your eyes light up. If you didn't care about us, you'd have left a long time ago."

"Got no room for caring in my life," he said, turning away from me. "Caring softens a man, makes him do things he wouldn't do otherwise. If a man softens, he can get himself put in a pine box real easy."

"If you don't care, then why stay?" I asked.

"Don't know exactly," he said. "Maybe it's just easier than riding away."

"Deacon's fast," I said, frowning. "Dunstan wouldn't've brought him down if he wasn't faster than you are. You could still ride off."

"No, son, I couldn't," he said. "As a man gets older, all he's got left is his pride. Jack Fletcher could have ridden off, but Billy Starr never ran from anybody."

"Which one's the real you?" I asked.

161

"Don't know," he said. "I must have a dozen names. I was Ed Lacey last year in Cheyenne."

"What's your real name?"

"Does it matter?" he asked, looking at me with a strange sadness. "I thought it did when I was a boy back in Texas, but that was a different me. I guess it's only right I should have a different name now."

"I guess so," I said.

I loaded my pistol and fired again at the rocks. I blasted four of them again, but it wasn't gladness that filled my insides. I felt like I was spending a man's last hours with him, and there should have been something really important being said or done.

Back at the farm I set kettles of hot water to boiling. Tom and Willie helped carry the hot water, and we soon had a bath ready for Fletcher.

"What's all this?" he asked me.

"I figured you'd want to look your best," I said.

Soon he was in the tub, scrubbing himself and whistling old cattle tunes. My brothers and I huddled nearby.

"Feels mighty good to be here just now," the man told us. "You take baths regular, Willie?" he asked my smallest brother.

"You don't have to take a bath to be a cattleman, do you?" Willie asked.

"Makes it a good deal more pleasant for others," Fletcher said.

"I guess I could take one on Saturday nights," Willie said with a big frown.

"We go swimming down at the creek," Tom said. "That keeps us clean mostly."

"Not like a good scrub," Fletcher said.

"You want your razor, Mr. Fletcher?" I asked. "You want to shave?"

"Yeah," he said. "And bring soap and a looking

162

glass."

I brought the shaving things, and he looked at his chin.

"Life's strange," he said, laughing. "A boy can't wait to shave. Then it goes and gets to be a chore."

We watched as he shaved. He looked different, younger when he finished. There was a brightness to his face I'd missed before.

"Maybe you can come back one of these days and show me how to shave," I said to him.

"You?" Tom said, laughing. "Likely it'll be me first."

"Well, might be in a couple of years I'll be wandering through and look in on you," he said. "Now Tom, Willie, you run on into the house. I got some words for Eric."

"Do we have to?" Tom complained. "I want to watch you put on your gun."

"Get going," Fletcher said, and the two of the popped to their feet and raced off out of the barn.

"I'll get your clothes," I said, opening the trunk.

"The yellow shirt," he said. "The black trousers, the ones with the pockets."

I searched through the trunk, clanging the coins against each other. Then I pulled out the trousers and handed them over. He put on his clothes, fastening them so that they fit tight against his hips and chest. He seemed thinner, more muscular. There was a power in his movements, and I seemed paralyzed.

"Bring my boots, son," he said.

"Yes, sir," I told him, bringing them over.

He pulled on his stockings, then slipped his big brown Indian boots over his feet. Then he walked over and put the long-barreled gun in its holster and buckled on his gunbelt.

"Guess I'm ready, son," he said, walking backward

163

so that the sunlight flashed off the barrel of his gun. "What do you think?"

"I think I'd be scared of you," I said.

"You ought to be scared of any man who's faster with a gun," he said. "That's nothing to be ashamed of, either. It's nature's warning to you."

"Mama will have lunch ready soon," I said.

"Thanks, but I'll get something at the cantina," he told me.

"Not like Mama's cooking," I said.

"No, but I'd just as soon keep the good-byes between you and me."

"You're not going to tell the others?" I asked. "They won't like that."

"I know, son, but I just couldn't face your mother this morning."

"I know you knew her before," I said.

He didn't say anything.

"She wouldn't let you go into town if she remembered you, would she?" I asked.

"She couldn't keep me from doing what I have to do," he said. "But she'd have a heavy heart about it."

"Tell me," I said. "Who are you?"

"You'll know when you need to," he said.

"I'll saddle the horses," I told him.

"Just one horse," he said. "You're not going."

"Sure I am," I said, stomping my foot on the ground. "That's why I learned to shoot. Dunstan still has two other men plus himself. If you kill Deacon, they'll shoot you."

"Then that's the way it'll be," he said. "Eric, son, I don't want you there. I don't want you to see what's going to happen. Understand?"

"You'll come back by when it's all over, won't you?" I asked.

"No, son," he said. "I'll ride on toward Santa Fe."

164

"No, you won't," I said, shaking away a tear from my eye. "You figure you're going to die, don't you? You know they'll shoot you down like a dog in the street. You won't even have anybody there who cares."

" 'Spect so," he said sadly.

"I'll miss you, Mr. Fletcher," I said, running over and putting my shoulder up against him. "I'll remember you."

"I know that, son," he said. "Eric, if I had a son of my own, I couldn't be any prouder of him than I am of you. You're a tough kid, and you'll make a fine man."

He threw his leg over his saddle and pointed to his cavalry hat.

"Hand me my hat, Eric," he said.

I picked it up and held it out to him. He took it and put it on his head. Looking up at him, I saw he was a proud man going off to battle. It reminded me of the stories of knights in Mama's book about King Arthur. She'd read it to me when I was littler than Willie.

"When it's all done with, give your mother the chest," he said. "When she looks through it, she'll understand everything."

"Good-bye," I said, waving at him. "Good luck."

Fletcher took his hand and gave me a sharp salute. Then he spurred his horse, and it reared up in the air. In another minute he had galloped off over the horizon.

XIX

I walked slowly to the house. There was an uneasiness hanging in the air. The clouds seemed to block out the sun, and for a minute I thought the storm from the night before might return.

I walked inside the house and sat down at the supper table. Mama had baked a fresh loaf of bread, and Tom and Willie were busy eating dried beef and beans. The food smelled good to me, but I had no appetite. I played with my fork, and Mama put her hand on my shoulder.

"Isn't Mr. Fletcher coming to dinner?" she asked.

"He's gone," I said, looking up at her.

"Oh?" she said. "When?"

"A few minutes ago," I told her. "He said to tell everybody good-bye."

"He's gone to kill Dunstan," Tom said through a mouthful of bread and butter.

"I'll bet he kills him before Dunstan even get his gun out of the holster," Willie said.

"He hasn't gone to fight Dunstan," I said, looking at the floor. "Dunstan sent for a man from Santa Fe. He's really fast. Mr. Fletcher will probably get killed."

"He will not," Willie said. "He's the fastest."

"He said there's always somebody faster," I told them. "It's not going to be easy. I figure Dunstan's other men will be there, too."

"Dunstan hasn't got many men left," Tom said, laughing.

"How many does it take to shoot a man in the back?" I asked. "Mr. Fletcher said he wasn't coming back."

"You're sure about that, Eric?" Mama asked. "He seemed so at peace when I talked to him the other day. It seems hard to believe."

"I know," I said, hanging my head. "He wasn't here very long, but I'm going to miss him."

"Me, too," Willie said.

"And me," Tom said.

No one said anything after that for a long time. Then Mama turned to me and frowned.

"It won't help for you to starve yourself, Eric," she said. "He'll be fine."

"No, he won't," I said. "How can I eat knowing he's in town right now facing up to Dunstan for us?"

"It won't help anyone for you to make yourself sick," Mama said.

I looked up at her and sighed. I tried to get a bite of beef into my mouth, but it had no taste. I set down my fork and leaned back in my chair.

"Why don't you go take a walk outside?" Mama said, touching my shoulder with her soft hand. "It might help."

"Yes, ma'am," I said.

I left the house and walked out into the afternoon heat. Sweat began soaking through my shirt, and I sought the shelter of the barn. I walked inside, pausing only long enough to pat my horse on its head. Then I walked over to Fletcher's trunk and sat down beside it.

It wasn't locked, and I fought back the instinct to open it. Inside that trunk was the key to Fletcher, who he really was. I wanted to see what secret lay hidden under the gold coins. I wanted to know why he'd ridden into town to die for Mama, to die for me.

As I sat there, I remembered the things he'd said. Over and over again he'd spoken to me about himself, about his days on the Cimarron, about his days in the cavalry. He'd said so many things, given me so many of the pieces to his life, but I couldn't fit them together. There had always been something held back, something hidden away from me.

I lay back against a bale of hay and closed my eyes. I hadn't slept well the night before. Suddenly I was very tired, and I wanted to slip away into a world of dreams. But every single time I closed my eyes, I kept seeing Fletcher standing in the street ready to take on the evil Deacon. Dunstan and the others were laughing, and I couldn't stand it.

"I thought you might be in here," Mama said to me, sitting beside the hay bale. She took her hands and rubbed the tension out of my shoulders. I rested my head back and let her take my problems in her hands.

"I thought you said he wasn't coming back," Mama said. "His trunk is still here."

"I know," I said, frowning.

"You know?" she asked, turning my chin so that I could look into her eyes. "Then why'd he leave his things?"

"Because he doesn't plan to be alive tomorrow," I said, trying to keep my eyes clear of tears.

"What are you talking about, Eric?" she asked. "Did he tell you that?"

"No, Mama," I said. "I don't know what's happening. I thought I had it all figured out. He's talked a lot about where he's been, what he's done, but I don't know where all the pieces fit."

"The pieces?" Mama asked.

"Mama, haven't you noticed anything about him? Hasn't something seemed familiar?"

"What do you mean?"

"He knew you before," I said. "I'm sure of it. He grew up along the Brazos River. He used to hunt buffalo with the Comanches."

"He told you he knew me?" she asked.

"No, ma'am," I said. "I figured that much. He kept asking about you. When I told him you were from Jacksboro, he started asking all sorts of questions. He asked about where you met Papa. He saw the wedding picture. He knew it was taken in Palo Pinto."

"You're sure?"

"Yes, Mama, I'm sure. When he went into town to fight Johnson, he showed me some things in the trunk. There are a bunch of gold coins in there. I don't know how much, but it looks like a lot of money to me. He said you'd be able to tell me all about why he had to go into town alone."

"I'd be able to tell you?" she asked. "I don't understand."

"That's what he said, Mama. He said if he got away from Johnson, he'd send word where to send the trunk. He didn't say anything like that this time."

"Eric, listen to me," she said. "Tell me exactly what he said about his family. Did he say anything about brothers?"

"He told me they all died when they were little, like Michael."

Mama frowned when I mentioned Michael, and I was sorry I mentioned his name.

"And his parents?" she asked, wiping her eyes.

"His father wasl killed in the war," I said. "I don't guess he had anywhere to go."

"I don't remember anyone like that," she said. "We didn't have all that many boys in the county, and most of them came back."

"Mama, we can look in the trunk," I said. "There has to be something in there."

"But you said you already saw the trunk," she said.

"Only the things on top," I said. "There were some things in the bottom. A box of some kind."

"Let's look," she said.

I opened the lid of the trunk and waited for her to sift through the things. On top were some buckskin trousers, a heavy buffalo coat, several shirts, stockings and other clothes. Mama stacked them neatly beside the trunk on a bale of hay.

"Here are the coins, Mama," I said, handing her a bag of gold pieces.

"Eric, there's a fortune here," she said. "Where'd he get so much money?"

"Mining," I said, looking at a deed. "This paper says it's the title to a land claim, Mama. There's a book in here that says thousands of dollars are in a Denver bank."

"Why leave it all here for us?" she asked.

"I don't know," I said, shaking my head.

I took out a gray uniform. It bore the insignia of a cavalry major. There were rips in the trouser legs, and the fabric was worn in many places. It had been kept clean, though, and it meant something to Fletcher. Beneath the uniform was a long cavalry saber. Engraved on the scabbard was a silver star with the seal of Texas on it.

"I never saw such a fine sword," I said, showing it to Mama.

"The Republic of Texas made several like this," she told me. "A man in New Orleans forged them. My father had one. It was something he put great stock in."

I took out three pistols. One was an army Colt. The others were custom built. The sights had been filed off, and they were light to my touch. They all had one thing in common, the balance was perfect.

"Look at this, Eric," Mama said, pulling out a blue flag with a single star in the center of it.

"What's that?" I asked.

"A regimental flag," she said. "It's from a volunteer regiment of Texas cavalry."

"Here's the box, Mama," I said, pulling it out.

She took it and opened it up. It was filled with letters, and she opened one. As she read, a tear wove its way down her cheek, and she choked.

"What is it, Mama?" I asked.

"A letter from his mother," she said.

"Does it say his name?"

"No," she said, "it doesn't have to."

"You know who he is?" I asked, my eyes growing wide.

Before she could answer, I spotted a small yellow photograph. When I held it to the light, I was stunned.

"Mama, look," I said. "The girl on the left. It's you!"

She took the photograph and looked at it. Tears flowed down her cheeks, and she leaned against my shoulder.

"Who is he, Mama?" I asked. "I don't understand."

"It can't be possible," she said, shaking her head.

"Mama, who is he?" I asked, standing up.

"Sit down, Eric," she said, taking my hand. "You

171

remember all the stories I told you about your Uncle
Sam Delamer?"

"Sure, Mama," I said.

"And of your Uncle Jamie?"

"He's the one who's a lawyer," I said.

"Well, Eric, I had another brother," she told me.

"I know all that," I said, impatient. "He's the one
Willie was named after. He died in the war."

"He didn't die," she said, squeezing my hand.

I turned back to the trunk, looking at the initials
W. D. Willie Delamer.

"He's my uncle?" I asked. "Why didn't he tell me?"

"Eric, it's not an easy thing to understand," she
said. "My brother Sam never got along too well with
Willie. Sam was driven by a need to build. Willie was
a wanderer. He used to spend the summers with the
Indians. He'd skip school whenever he could get
away with it."

"I'll bet he caught it good for that," I said.

"Nobody could ever punish Willie," she said. "He
was special. He never frowned. He'd run and play
and laugh and shout. If he got hurt, he'd never show
it. Papa loved him more than anyone. Mama, too.
Willie understood all about the Indians, all about the
people who'd lived along the river before we came.

"Papa never said anything, but he always figured
the land would pass to Willie. Willie got along with
everyone. The Indian wars never would have happened if Willie had stayed in the valley. But when
Papa rode off to war, Willie went with him."

"Grandpapa Delamer was a hero, wasn't he?" I
asked.

"We'd fought in a couple of wars, Eric. He was
killed that first spring against the Yankees."

"And Uncle Willie?"

"Willie and I were close, Eric, close like you and

172

Tom. We wrote a lot back and forth. Then his letters lost their glow. The old Willie sort of died."

"He told me it was the killing," I said sadly. "He said his family was all killed off by the war."

"I guess in a way they were," Mama said. "When it was all over, Sam made it very plain that Willie wasn't welcome. The ranch was Sam's now, and Willie didn't belong. I got a few letters from him. Then a letter came saying he'd been killed in a gun battle up on the Cimarron River."

"How come he didn't tell us who he was, Mama?" I asked.

"I guess he knew I wouldn't let him go," she said. "He's not my little brother anymore, though. He's a grown man."

"He's gone off to die," I said, sighing. "I never even had a chance to know he was my uncle. I never told him thanks for taking up for me."

"Eric, do you suppose it's too late?" she asked.

"I don't know," I said. "They'll wait for the sun to get straight up so there are no shadows."

"Then get your horse saddled and go into town."

"Ma'am?" I asked. "I don't understand."

"Do you still have your father's pistol?" she asked.

"Yes, ma'am," I said.

"Can you fire it? Can you hit something with it?"

"Sure," I said. "Not like I can with a rifle, but I can shoot. Can't draw yet. Fletcher . . . I mean Uncle Willie was going to teach me."

"Now listen carefully, Eric," she said. "This is what I want you to do. Get an egg basket. Cover it with a napkin. Slip the pistol under the napkin. Then get down to town."

"Yes, ma'am," I said.

"I want you to watch Dunstan. If he makes even a slight move for his gun, you shoot him."

173

"You mean shoot him dead?" I asked.

"Dead!" she said. "He didn't give your father a chance. I don't know much about shooting men, but I know Dunstan. He'll shoot Willie in the back if he has a chance."

"Mama, what if I can'd do it?" I asked. "I've never looked a man in the eye and shot him. I fired off my rifle at that man down by the barn, but that was different."

"Just keep this in mind, Eric," she said. "That man in the street's your uncle. He's standing there so you won't have to.

"No man in our family's ever shirked his duty. I know it's a man's job you'll be doing, but you're the only one who can do it. No one'll be surprised if you show up down there, and Dunstan won't give a second thought to you."

"You're right, Mama," I said. "Besides, Dunstan won't even be in the gunfight."

"Don't you believe that, son," she said. "You just do what I say. Keep your eyes on Dunstan."

"Yes, ma'am," I said, starting to saddle my horse.

When I finally led the horse out of the barn, Mama was waiting outside. She threw her arms around me and hugged me tight.

"Be careful, Eric," she said.

"Mama, what if . . . what if . . ."

"Nothing's going to happen, Eric," she said. "Even if it did, we'd make out fine. I can handle a rifle, you know, and Tom's good around the farm. We'll be just fine."

As I climbed into the saddle, Tom and Willie ran out and gathered around me.

"You going into town?" Tom asked.

"Yes," I said, taking the egg basket Mama handed me.

Tom's smile fell from his face when he saw I had Papa's pistol. He looked up into my eyes and tried not to frown. He couldn't bring himself to say anything, but he grabbed my hand and clutched it firmly.

Willie jumped up behind me in the saddle and rode with me to the front gate. He patted me on the back, and I hugged him. Then he slid off the back of the horse, and I rode on toward town, alone.

XX

It was a different me who rode to town. I was puzzled a little earlier. Now everything fit. The man I'd known as Fletcher was really my own uncle. He was fighting Dunstan for my mother, for me, for Tom and Willie.

I looked overhead at the sun. It was climbing higher and higher into the sky. I knew the time was coming quickly when I would have to decide whether to be a boy or a man. I found myself gripping Papa's pistol tightly and sitting as tall as I could in the saddle. That didn't make me a man, though, and I shuddered to think of facing Dunstan's deadly eyes, waiting for the man to try to shoot my uncle.

I glanced back over my shoulder at our farm. I saw Mama and my brothers waving at me from the fence. It was for them that it was all about. I swallowed deeply and frowned. A hardness came to my insides, and I kicked the horse into a gallop. A long line of dust swirled up from behind me, and it was but a short while later that I arrived in town.

An eerie silence hung in the air. Front Street was deserted. Only the sound of loose boards rattling in the wind could be heard. Nothing but a solitary tumbleweed moved in the street.

Uncle Willie stood in the door of the cantina. I drew my horse to a halt and looked at him. His eyes appeared brighter, younger. There was less anger in his face. He seemed filled with a strange kind of calm. He didn't seem nervous at all. It was as if he didn't know what was about to happen.

I slid down from the saddle and led my horse to the hitching rack beside his own mount. As I tied the reins to the wooden post, I looked at him a second time. I could tell by the scowl on his face that he had seen me.

I walked slowly to his side. Every step I took brought a deeper frown to his face. My feet felt heavy. It hurt to know I was bringing him pain.

I stood in front of him for several minutes before he even looked at me. It was as if there was a fifty foot wall between us, one I couldn't break down. When I finally felt his hand on my shoulder, I looked into his glaring eyes.

"I asked you to stay home, Eric," he said, turning away from me. "I don't want you here."

"I know," I said, frowning. "But everything's changed. I know all about you. Mama looked in your trunk. It was her idea that I come."

He looked back at me, a trace of confusion in his eyes.

"How come you didn't tell me?" I asked. "There's so much I want to say, and now there's no time."

"Does it really change anything?" he asked. "It would have been easier on both of us if your mother hadn't told you until tomorrow."

"Would it have been?" I asked. "I watched them gun down Papa. I couldn't do a thing about it. Maybe I can help this time."

"Help?" he asked, laughing.

I leaned over against him and whispered, "I've got Papa's gun in the egg basket," I pointed to the basket hooked on my saddle horn. "It was Mama's idea to bring it. I'm supposed to watch Dunstan."

"Dunstan?" he said, his forehead wrinkling. "You keep clear of that man."

"I promised Mama," I told him. "I have to watch him. If he reaches for his gun, I'll blast him."

"And if you miss?"

"I don't suppose he will," I said, looking at my feet.

"Look, Eric. I appreciate what you're trying to do, but this is something for me to do," he told me. "It's what I do best. I never was good at growing things like your mother. I never was good at building things like your father. But when it comes to fighting, there's never been a man my equal."

"You can't fight them all," I said.

"You're wrong, Eric," he said. "I've done it before. I've been fighting somebody for as long as I can remember. First it was Yankees. Then it was gunmen. Up in Montana I fought Sioux Indians. North of Denver I fought mine pirates. Leave the fighting to me. You get on your horse and go home."

"I can't," I said. "When I was little, Mama used to say I reminded her of her brother Willie. I can fight, too. I'm not scared of them, you know. I won't miss."

He looked into my eyes for a long minute. Then he smiled. Holding out his hand, he drew me to him and reached a big arm around me.

"You'll grow into a good man, Eric, if the world just gives you time," he said. "Now get yourself off this street."

I looked up at him and watched a smile come to his lips. Then I walked back to my horse and took the egg basket down. In another minute I'd found shelter behind a corner of the barber shop.

That was when Deacon finally walked out into the street. Dunstan's other two men stood in the doorway of the saloon. Dunstan himself walked across the street and sat down not fifteen feet from where I was hiding. The man had his eyes on my uncle's back, and I shook uncontrollably.

Mama had told me to keep my eyes on Dunstan, but just that moment I was watching Deacon. He was wearing his shirt with the pearl buttons and a fancy silk sash. He looked more like one of those traveling actors than a hired killer.

Deacon had a broad smile on his face as he walked into the center of Front Street. His white teeth sparkled in the sunlight, and his eyes were bright, excited. I could tell he was one of those men who enjoyed the killing, thrived on it.

I held my egg basket out so that I could see Papa's pistol underneath the napkin. I felt like a fool. I hadn't ever brought an egg basket to town before. Nobody seemed to notice, though. Dunstan's eyes were fixed on the two gunmen as they turned in half circles opposite each other in the center of the street.

"Well, I thought maybe you'd be on the morning train to Denver," Deacon said, spitting on the ground. "Thought you might have given a little thought to living a little longer."

"You know how it is, Deacon," Uncle Willie said, gazing at the man with his cold eyes. "You don't run away from death. It has a way of catching up to you."

"It does at that," Deacon said, laughing. "I never faced a man who seemed like he was ready before," the man said with an evil smile. "Guess it's better to die that way."

"Die?" Uncle Willie said, laughing so that the

street echoed with the sound. "I won't be the one dying here this day. You're the dead man, Deacon, you and them," he said, pointing to Dunstan's men in the doorway of the saloon.

"This is just between you and me," Deacon said.

"You think you're good, don't you?" Uncle Willie asked. "You know what Dunstan thinks of you? He figures you'll keep me busy for a minute. Then those two can kill me. You're just what we called cannon fodder back in Virginia."

Deacon turned and looked back at the two men.

"Leave!" Deacon shouted at the men.

The two stood frozen. It was as if they were nailed to the floor.

"You two listen to me," Uncle Willie said. "If I'm still standing when we finish this, you're dead men. You think about that a moment. You think about whether Dunstan's paying you enough to get yourself killed."

The two men exchanged looks. One of them seemed nervous, but the other grabbed his arm. They both stayed there.

"Well, Deacon?" Uncle Willie said. "You see what I mean?"

"Doesn't matter," Deacon said, spitting again. "They won't have nothing left to do."

"That's true enough," Uncle Willie said. "They'll be as dead as you'll be."

"Or you," Deacon said, laughing.

"It doesn't matter to me," Uncle Willie said, glancing a second at me. "I don't really care anymore. How about you, Deacon? You ready to die?"

"Don't plan to," Deacon said.

"You're not answering me, are you?" Uncle Willie asked. "You'd best think it over a minute before you make your play. You'd best think about how you're spending your last day on this earth. You look around and remember the sunrise. You try to remember the last girl you kissed. You remember how you looked into my eyes and saw the man who killed you."

"Never heard you were a talker, Starr," Deacon said, beginning to shake slightly. "Always figured you for a doer."

"I'll get done by and by," Uncle Willie said.

"We going to stand here jawing all day?" Deacon shouted.

"Just waiting for the sun to get itself on up in the sky," Uncle Willie said. "Getting nervous?"

Deacon glanced around the street. The air was deathly still. Nothing moved. The smile fell from Deacon's lips. A cloud moved across the sky, blocking out the sun and casting a shadow across the street.

Deacon spit again, then began laughing.

"Long as we're waiting. I believe I'll try a cigar," Deacon said, moving his hand.

"You'd best take that cigar from your pocket with the other hand, Deacon," Uncle Willie said. "I'd sure hate to kill a man for smoking a cigar."

"That would be a fine thing," Deacon said, laughing. "And after Mr. Dunstan shelled out all this lovely money for me to kill you."

Deacon lit the cigar and took a deep puff on it.

"Nothing like a good cigar," Deacon said.

"Enjoy it while you can," Uncle Willie said.

The two gunfighters suddenly stared hard at each other. The cloud moved, and sunlight blazed down on the street. The wind seemed to sigh in a haunting sort of way. I clutched the splintery side of the barber shop as Deacon threw his cigar on the ground. Then Deacon blinked, and I felt myself tremble.

It only took a second for the two men to pull their revolvers. I watched Deacon as the excitement raced across his face. I saw his fingers draw the pistol level and prepare to fire it. Then a single flash of surprise filled his eyes as a shot rang out. A red spurt of blood burst forth from Deacon's forehead, and his eyes grew cloudy. For a second Deacon seemed to be frozen in a strange dance of death. Then the man's legs buckled, and he fell to the ground.

Part of me wanted to scream out with joy, but it wasn't over. Uncle Willie rolled across the ground, as a shot rang out from the saloon. One of Dunstan's men, a man named Bond, leaped out into the street and fired. The bullets kicked up pillars of dust behind Uncle Willie's legs, but my uncle managed to crawl behind a watering trough.

Bond and the other man were spraying the street with bullets now, and I hugged the side of the building. One part of me wanted to rush out into the street and help, but the other part of me was terrified. Then I remembered what Mama said. Watch Dunstan.

The man was standing a few feet from me. He was smiling, watching, laughing to himself. I hated him, I wanted to take out the gun and shoot him right then, but my hand was paralyzed.

I heard Bond shout something, and the two men rushed out into the street. The man to Bond's right suddenly stumbled and fell. Blood covered his shirt.

Bond kept going. He was almost on top of Uncle Willie. Bond fired, and my uncle fell back hard against the porch of the mercantile. As he fell, Uncle Willie fired twice into Bond's smiling face, chasing the smile away forever.

I bolted out into the street, leaving my fear behind. I ran straight to Uncle Willie, sliding to the ground beside him. His shoulder was soaked in blood, and he was reaching with his right hand for his gun.

"It's all right," I said, tearing a strip from my shirt to use as a bandage. "You got all three of them."

"Eric," Uncle Willie started to say.

"Everything's going to be fine," I told him. "We'll get you back to the farm, and Mama will take the bullet out."

There was something in his eyes that stopped my talking. It wasn't a warning exactly. It was a look of despair mixed with fear. It was then that I heard footsteps on the porch of the mercantile, and I remembered Mama's warning. Watch Dunstan.

I knew without looking that Dunstan was standing behind us. When I glanced up at last, he smiled his cruel way and waved his Colt revolver in my face.

"What's that you got there, boy?" he asked. "That in your hands."

"An egg basket," I said, putting it aside long enough to press my makeshift bandage against Uncle Willie's bullet wound.

"Not much point to that," Dunstan said, pushing my hand away. "He's what you might call living on borrowed time. Now what's this egg basket business. I never seen you carry eggs in all your life."

He kicked the egg basket, and Papa's pistol rolled out one side. Dunstan smiled again, then kicked the pistol halfway across the street.

"A fine mess you got yourself into, Starr" Dunstan said. "If you'd had a man backing you up, you'd have me dead on the porch of the barber shop. This boy'd be taking you home to his mama. Got to admit, you took Deacon real easy. I figured he'd put at least one hole in you."

"Let the boy go, Mike," Uncle Willie said.

"He won't stay little forever," Dunstan said. "I

figure he must've come close to shooting me today. Next time he might."

I shuddered. My lip quivered as I realized what Dunstan was talking about.

"Move aside, boy," Dunstan said.

I drew back, gazing intently into the eyes of the man who stood there pointing a gun at my uncle. There was no excitement, no relish for killing in those eyes. It was the same businesslike Dunstan I'd seen a hundred times before.

"Get over there on the other side of that watering trough," Dunstan said to me.

"Do what he says, Eric," Uncle Willie told me.

I circled the trough, noticing that Bond's discarded pistol lay hidden at my feet.

"Well, Starr it's come to this," Dunstan said. "You're still soft, you know. I'd never've gotten myself into this position. I'd have gone for the top man right off, shot him down. You forget what I taught you on the Cimarron. Always go for the head. The arms don't matter much once the head's gone."

I tried to control my shivering as I watched the blood flowing from the wound in Uncle Willie's shoulder. His eyes were growing dim and watery. His face was full of death.

"Get it over with, Mike," my uncle told him.

"In my own good time," Dunstan said, laughing. "It's my turn to do the talking now."

"No, your time's up," Uncle Willie told him. "These people know you can be taken."

"These people?" Dunstan asked, spitting on the ground beside Uncle Willie's head. "If a single one of them had any guts, he'd be out here pumping lead into me this minute."

They stared at each other a minute, and I kicked the pistol out where I could get to it. I planned what to do. I'd have to dive to the ground, then blast away before Dunstan knew what was happening. But as I tried to muster the courage to do it, my whole body took to shaking.

Uncle Willie figured it out. I saw his cold stare warn me, try to tell me to get away. But we both knew I was all there was, the only one who could help either one of us.

"The people in this town would sell their mother to stay alive," Dunstan went on to say. "And when they see I don't mind shooting a kid, they'll give me anything I want."

"The boy's got family in Texas," Uncle Willie said. "I gave you a week. You owe me."

"You're dead 'cause you got sentimental, Starr. Not me."

Dunstan swung his gun over and cocked it. He put it right in Uncle Willie's face, and I coughed.

"Don't make the kid watch, Mike," Uncle Willie begged.

"Turn your head, boy," Dunstan said.

I knew then that I'd have only one chance. I turned my head and bent down. Taking the gun in my right hand, I swung around and fired at Dunstan. The bullet blasted the window of the mercantile, and Dunstan turned toward me. I pulled the trigger a second time as Dunstan fired a bullet into my shoulder. We both tumbled backward and fell.

I felt my chest numb with pain, and I couldn't move my left arm at all. I crawled forward to see Dunstan, but I came to look into Uncle Willie's eyes first.

"You done fine, Eric," he said to me.

I tried to stand up, but my head was light, and sticky blood covered the whole left side of my body.

"What's this boy to you, Starr?" Dunstan whispered hoarsely as I reappeared in his sight. "Who is he?"

"Nothing much," Uncle Willie said.

"To be shot down by a dumb kid not old enough to shave," Dunstan said, coughing blood from his mouth. Then Dunstan slumped forward, dead.

"Uncle Willie?" I said, reaching out for him. "I'm cold."

I never heard if he answered. I felt numb all over, and darkness crept over me. All I knew was an eerie silence, and I found myself floating. Then there was nothing at all.

XXI

I woke up in my bed back on the farm. My whole body was stiff, and when I tried to sit up, my head starting spinning. I looked up at the ceiling a minute, then glanced around the room. Daylight was seeping into the room through the window.

I didn't understand what was happening. I couldn't remember anything after the gunfight. Then I turned my head and looked at my shoulder. It was bound tight with bandages, and the flesh around it was colored a sickly white.

I managed to raise myself slowly so that I was sitting up in my bed. My head was still dizzy, but it cleared in a few minutes. I listened for the sound of my brothers, for Mama, for anyone at all, but there was nothing. The house was quiet as a churchyard.

"Mama," I called out faintly.

I heard a rush of feet, and Mama poked her head through the door.

"Thank God," she said, rushing to my side. "Eric, I've been so worried."

"What happened?" I asked.

"Don't you remember anything?" she asked. "You were shot."

"I remember that part," I said. "But how'd I get here? I thought I was dead."

"Mr. Roderick picked you up and carried you into his house. Dr. Wilson came by and took the bullet out. You bled like a pig in a slaughterhouse, but you're fine now. Mr. Roderick probably saved your life."

"How long have I been out?" I asked.

"The better part of two days," she said. "We took turns watching you, Tom and I. Even Willie watched you some. I wanted to be here when you woke up."

"It doesn't matter," I said. "Help me get up."

"Not today," she told me. "You just lie back and rest, son. There's nothing to worry about. You saw to that."

"I saw to that?"

"You did just what I told you to do. You shot Dunstan. You weren't too clever about it, I know, but you got the job done."

"I killed him?"

"Yes, Eric," she said.

I slumped back into the bed and died a little inside.

"Hey, it's nothing to feel low about," Mama said, stroking my good shoulder. "He was a bad man. He held a gun on your uncle."

"I know," I said, swallowing a sob, "but does it really make a difference? I mean I did kill a man. It's not like killing a rattlesnake or a wolf."

"Yes, it is," she said. "That man was just like a wolf. He surely didn't do any grieving after your father was killed. He didn't hesitate when he shot down the sheriff."

"Mama, I was so scared," I said. "Uncle Willie was brave, and I couldn't even help. I just stood there and watched."

"You did what mattered when you needed to," she said.

"But I could have shot Bond," I said, turning away from her. "Then Uncle Willie wouldn't even have been hurt."

"And you'd have gotten yourself killed, Eric," she told me. "That's the one thing Willie would never have been able to bear."

"And Uncle Willie?" I asked. "How is he?"

She frowned and walked to the door.

"We'll talk of that later," she said, glancing back at me. "When you're feeling better."

"Now," I said.

"Not now," she said, shaking her head. "You won't want to hear what I have to say just now."

I looked into her sad eyes and tried not to cry. She left a few minutes later, and Tom walked in. He sat down at the foot of the bed and looked me over.

"I thought you weren't ever going to wake up, Eric," he told me. "You were sure bloody when they brought you here."

"Who brought me?" I asked.

"The doc and Mr. Roderick," he said. "Eric, everybody in town's talking about the way you shot Dunstan. You're a hero."

"I don't want to be a hero," I said.

"You don't?" Tom asked, surprised.

"No, I just want things to be the way they used to be. I want Papa back. I don't ever want to see a gun again!"

"Can I have Papa's Colt then?" Tom asked excitedly.

"No!" I said. "Tom, you don't understand what it's like. You look into a man's eyes. One minute they're full of life. Then you pull the trigger, and those eyes are cold, dead. All the brightness that was there is gone."

"You still feeling dizzy?" he asked.

"No," I said, "it's just that I've done it now, Tom. Nothing's ever going to be the same again."

Willie walked in and sat down on the bed beside me. I patted him on the back, and he hugged my arm. It hurt my sore shoulder, but I was glad he'd done it. I needed to feel somebody close just then.

"You keeping the cows tended?" I asked Tom.

"Sure, Eric," my oldest brother said. "We were down at the creek checking the fences this morning. Everything's just fine. Most of the people from the farms have been coming by paying Mama for the seed and such they bought off you the other day. We're going to be fine. No more eating wild turnips."

"No more turnips," I said, laughing at the thought.

"The doc'll be by after a while," Tom said. "You ought to see your shoulder. Doc Wilson isn't too neat, you know. He made a pretty ugly scar there."

"There go my looks," I said.

"Looks?" Tom asked, laughing at me. "What looks?"

"You just wait till I can get up," I said. "I'll thrash you but good."

"That'll be just fine with me," Tom said, growing serious. "Willie and I miss you, Eric. There's a lot more work to get done, and we don't seem to have any fun nowadays. I even miss your feet kicking me around in bed."

"Then help me get up," I said. "I'm tired of lying around here."

"Mama would have a fit," Tom said, backing away from me. "You want to play cards?"

"All right," I said, grumbling to myself, "you'll have to deal, though."

"Fine with me," Tom said. "It's easier to cheat that way."

I looked at him and tried to frown. But the laughter that danced across his face reminded me of a hundred good times we'd had in the past, and I laughed back at him. I laughed even though the laughter sent shivers of pain through my shoulder.

"Are you all right?" Tom asked as I winced.

"Sure," I said.

We played several hands at cards before Willie came running in. He walked up and looked down on me in my bed. Saying nothing, he put his hand beside me and smiled.

"It's good to see you," I told him, patting his little back with my good hand.

"Doc's here," Willie announced. "Mama said to tell Tom to go feed the chickens."

"Well, that's all the cards for now," I said. "Come back when the doc leaves."

"We will," Tom said. "Mama's cooking some steaks for supper. Mr. Hazard sent them over. She's been baking peach pie, too."

"I wish I was hungry," I said.

They walked out of the room as Dr. Wilson came inside. He began cutting away the bandages, humming to himself some song he must have heard in a saloon. Mama didn't like him much, but he was the only doctor around. When I saw my shoulder, I frowned. He'd cut a great jagged tear into the flesh, not at all the careful cut Mama had made in Uncle Willie's leg.

"Got yourself a fine scar there, young man," the doctor told me.

"Yes, sir," I said. "I guess you took the bullet out of my uncle, too."

"Your uncle?" the doctor asked.

I saw the confusion on his face. No one had been told who the man called Fletcher really was.

"I called him that," I said. "Mr. Fletcher."

"I never saw the man," the doctor said.

"But you had to," I said. "We were there together."

"Look, son, I promised your mother I wouldn't speak of this," Dr. Wilson said. "She was afraid you'd be upset."

"He's dead," I said, looking away from him.

The doctor said nothing further. He drained the wound and put on clean bandages. Then the man left, and I stared at the ceiling.

Mama came in a few minutes later and sat down at the foot of my bed. There was a sadness on her face, and I waited for her to speak.

"He loved you very much, Eric," she told me. "I don't believe he would have done what he did for anyone else."

"That makes it worse," I said. "Mama, it's all my fault."

"Eric, Willie was always alone. He came and went through this country without tasting the joys of living. He never belonged. You gave him something priceless. For just a little while he belonged here. I think he needed that."

"Mama, what happened? He wasn't shot any worse than me."

"Maybe it was age, Eric. Maybe it was just not caring anymore. I don't know," she said, turning her head so that I couldn't see her eyes. "You know everyone needs a fresh start, son."

"A fresh start?" I asked, confused.

"Sometimes death can bring more peace than life, Eric. I don't think Willie ever had much peace in his life. Maybe he'll find some now."

"Did he say something, Mama?" I asked. "Did he say anything before he . . . before he . . . died?"

"Only a few things," she said. "Mainly that he loved us. And Eric, he asked me to tell you to remember the face of the man you killed. He said never to forget. Whenever you get angry, whenever you start to pull out a gun, remember how you felt when you shot Dunstan."

"I could never forget," I said, shaking with horror.

"Well, I'd best bring you some supper in. Eric, he's at peace now. Keep that thought close to your heart."

"Peace?" I asked, swallowing some of my sadness. "What's peace?"

Mama didn't try to answer. She walked into the front room and started laying out dinner. When she brought me my supper, I picked at it. I couldn't find any appetite. Mama came back in a few minutes later and frowned.

"I thought you'd like the dinner," she said.

"I don't have much appetite," I said.

193

"You can't let it bother you," she said, wrinkling her forehead. "It doesn't make sense to you right now, but tomorrow you'll feel better."

"Tomorrow?" I asked.

"Reverend Manchester's coming out tomorrow to read over him," Mama said. "You can pray for him then, Eric. He'd like that, I think."

"Maybe he would," I said.

That night after Tom and Willie had climbed into the bed they had to share, I slid from under my blankets and stood up on the floor. I was still dizzy, and I grabbed the bed to keep from falling. When I got my balance, I stumbled out of the room and made my way through the front door to the porch.

For a few minutes I just wandered around the open ground in front of the house. Then my eyes looked up into the sky, and I knew why I'd come.

The sky was filled with a thousand stars that night, and every single one of them seemed to be shining down especially for me. I felt a closeness to the night air, and I guess what Mama would have called peace came to me. I leaned against the front post that sheltered the steps and sighed.

I hadn't felt so sad since the night after Papa died. I stayed up all night beside the coffin, talking to Papa like he was still alive. There was no coffin to talk to now, and only the emptiness kept me company.

"Why?" I asked, staring at the brilliant moon. "I don't understand."

No voice broke through the stillness to bring my answer. I sat down and listened to the crickets beyond the garden. A hoot owl spoke his haunting words to me from behind the barn. I felt a tear

194

roll down my cheek.

"It's all my fault," I whispered to the owl. "I wish I'd never met him."

But it was a lie. I'd prayed for him to come. Now there would be no other man to ride through my life, stand in my place when danger confronted my family. From now on I would have to face life alone, by myself.

"He was a hard man," I said quietly, praying more with my heart than with my words. "I know he killed a lot of men, but that wasn't the man I knew. God, remember him like I will. He smiled when you got to know him, and he was kind to a boy once. That ought to count for something."

I wiped from my eyes the moisture which would have been tears a week or a month before. Then I got my feet in motion and made my way back to bed. I didn't sleep much, though.

XXII

It was not a bright morning. The sky was black, streaked with the first rays of sunlight. Thunder rumbled somewhere in the distance, and off and on it rained. There was a strange chill in the air, almost unheard-of for August.

I stood on the porch dressed in my Sunday clothes, sandwiched in between my brothers Tom and Willie. Mama was behind us, shaking her head sadly at the weather.

"It'll be raining by nine o'clock," she said. "I hate funerals in the rain."

Tom and Willie nodded their heads in agreement, but I didn't. It seemed right and proper to me that a funeral should take place on such a day. I couldn't've faced a sunrise full of color just then. My face was as gloomy as the sky, and my insides were frozen with grief.

Tom and Willie walked to the barn to get the wagon. Mama didn't mind riding, being raised on a horse ranch and all, but she insisted on taking the wagon. I knew it was because she didn't figure I was strong enough to ride a horse. She just didn't want to remind me of my shoulder or the gunfight.

I almost smiled as Tom tried to keep Willie from stepping in the small puddles. Mama winced every time Willie muddied himself. She'd made us all scrub ourselves raw in the bathtub, then put on our best clothes. We hadn't looked any better for Papa's burying.

Tom and Willie disappeared into the barn, and I could hear the horses complaining as my brothers began the harnessing. Saddle horses don't take to pulling wagons, and I wished I'd been well enough to help. Tom had never had my way with horses, and Willie teased them too often.

"Whatever is taking so long?" Mama asked, stirring nervously. "You'd think they could hitch up a wagon."

"They can, Mama," I said, looking up at her.

"I'm sorry, Eric," she said, putting her arms around my chest. "I didn't mean to complain."

I said nothing. I saw in her face the same red eyes, the same sadness I knew could be found on my own.

"I'm sad, too," I said, hugging her. "I wish Papa was here."

"So do I, Eric," she said. "And Willie, too."

Tom and Willie brought the wagon out finally, and Tom climbed down to help me into the back. I sat down on a saddle blanket with Willie. Tom took the reins and joined Mama on the seat.

"Take your time getting us there, Tom," Mama said. "No one hurries to a funeral."

"Yes, ma'am," Tom answered.

We did ride slowly to the small hill where Papa

197

and Michael and Elsa lay buried. There was a fourth white cross there now, made from fence pickets by Tom to mark Uncle Willie's grave. They'd buried him right after the gunfight, but Mama postponed the funeral until Reverend Manchester could come out and read over the grave. You didn't wait to bury a body in summer. The smell's powerful after a few hours.

I figured maybe Mama wanted to wait on account of me, too. She knew I wouldn't be up for a few days, and she thought it was important for me to go. Me, I hated the idea that Uncle Willie was dead, and going to a funeral wouldn't much help.

When we got to the hill, the rain grew worse. Willie huddled against me for shelter, and Mama drew her shawl up tight against her ears. The townspeople who'd come moved around impatiently, and Reverend Manchester began by reading some words from his Bible. Then he turned toward Mama.

"I didn't know the man we're praying over this morning," the reverend began. "Most of us here didn't know him. I'm told he wasn't a man known by many. Those who did know him say he had a gentleness to him others didn't see."

The reverend paused, nodded to Mama, then continued. I felt Mama squeeze my hand as his words flowed.

"This man, who called himself Jack Fletcher, was a man of violence. He was a man who committed grave sins, terrible sins. There is no greater sin than the taking of a human life. He killed, often enough that men knew him more by the death that filled his heart than by even his name.

But as he lay dying, I'm told he prayed for forgiveness. A man who dies with a prayer upon his lips can find salvation. We're promised this, and it's a thought we should be ever mindful of.

"We didn't know much of this man. I'm told he fought in the war back East. War can twist a man, and I can't help but feel this was a twisted man. I've been told he fought in the cattle wars on the Cimarron River. A life of violence, my friends, can end no other way but in violence.

"I can't speak of the reasons for this man being the person he was. I only know he seemed to fight for right when the choice was given him. For this we are all thankful. We can only hope and pray that this man might find in death a peace he was denied in life."

I listened to the words. They hung heavily on my heart. I felt them weighing me down, crushing the life out of me. Every word he said was like a knife stabbing deep into my wounded heart.

"Eric, come with me," Mama whispered as the reverend read the final words of a funeral prayer.

"Yes, ma'am," I said, following her to the grave.

I swallowed tears as I walked past Papa and Michael. Then I knelt beside Mama as she said her silent words.

"Why'd the reverend call him Fletcher?" I whispered to Mama.

"I think if Willie'd wanted everyone to know, he'd have told them," she said. "I sat up with him for almost an hour, Eric. He said you'd know where he wanted to be buried, that you'd be able to explain it all. I remember what you said about paying for the land, and about sacrificing, about

199

belonging. I knew that was what Willie was talking about."

I didn't try to talk to her about it just then. I knew there'd be another time. Instead I stood with Mama and Tom and little Willie as the people came by and paid their respects.

"He was a violent man," old Mrs. Johnson told Mama. "I have no kind words for such as him."

"Then I'm sorry you came, Mrs. Johnson," Mama said. "A heart with no room for forgiveness is a very small heart."

Mrs. Johnson stormed off, but I found myself sharing a silent smile with Mama.

"How's the shoulder, boy?" Mr. Roderick asked me. "You figure you're ready to throw horseshoes yet?"

"No, sir," I said, trying to force a smile to my lips. "It hurts some, but we Sheidlers are tough."

"Are at that," the man said, shaking my hand.

The people seemed to melt away as the rain fell harder. Soon only Mama and we boys stood beside the simple white cross.

"I'll come back next week and carve his name on the cross," I said to Mama. "It should be on there."

"Why?" Mama asked. "Those who care will know, and those that don't, well, I don't see how it could matter to them."

"It matters to me," I said. "It belongs there."

"Then I expect Willie would have wanted you to carve it there," she said.

Mama led Willie back to the wagon, and they pulled a blanket over themselves to help battle the rain. I stood with Tom over the graves and frowned.

"Was he really our uncle, Eric?" Tom asked me.

"Sure was," I told him.

"How come he didn't say so?" Tom asked. "I mean, he should've said something. All those times we could've gone fishing and swimming. It wasn't right for him to go into town all alone."

"No," I said.

"He was brave, wasn't he, Eric?"

"He was brave," I said, echoing Tom's words.

"You suppose he got to heaven?"

"He should have," I said. "I figure he earned it. He sure didn't know much of heaven here on earth."

Tom walked away after a few more minutes, and I was left alone with the white crosses. I tried to think of what to say, but words failed me just then.

"Want to talk about it?" Mama asked me, her soft words chasing away some of the loneliness that had descended on me.

"Mama, I'll miss him," I told her. "He was really good to me."

"He loved you, Eric," she said. "I told you once that the two of you weren't really so alike. I was wrong. You both made your stands, just like your father and my grandfather who fought the Mexicans for Texas's independence. It wasn't an easy thing you did, but you did it."

"Can we go home now?" I asked.

"Are you tired?" she asked, feeling my forehead.

"It's not that," I said. "I just can't stand being here. It's like I'm strangling."

"I know what you mean," she said. "I hope this is our last trip here to read over a dead man."

201

"Me, too," I said. "We've paid enough for this land."

"Too much," Mama said, wiping a tear away from her eyes.

We rode back to the house in silence. After we'd gotten out of our wet clothes and dried our hair, Mama brought us to the table to enjoy a bowl of hot soup. While Tom and Willie washed the dinner dishes, Mama led me to the porch.

"It was a lovely service, wasn't it?" she asked.

"Yes, ma'am," I said.

"I liked what the reverend said about peace," she said, smiling. "I like to think of death that way."

"Me, too, Mama. It's what you were trying to say last night. But it's hard to feel good about people dying."

"It happens to everyone sooner or later," she told me, leading me to the edge of the porch so that we could sit down together.

"Mama, do you ever stop missing them, the people who die?" I asked her. "I still miss Papa and Michael. Even little Elsa, and she wasn't very big."

"You'll always miss them," Mama told me. "That's what being a family's all about. They were a part of you."

I nodded to her. I wondered if that was true. If it was, could you lose so many parts of you that you just dried up and blew away? Right then I felt like I'd lost about the last good part of me I had left.

"What's bothering you, Eric?" Mama asked. "You're not still blaming yourself for what happened?"

"It's not that, Mama. I was just thinking about what Reverend Manchester said. He said it's a terrible thing to kill a man. I killed Dunstan. Does that mean I've lost my soul?"

"No," she said, wrapping her arms around me. "It's a terrible thing to kill anyone, but sometimes we don't have any choice, Eric. There are always some men who force us to do things we don't want to do. Dunstan was like that. You didn't have any choice. He certainly would have killed you, did put a bullet into you. He was holding a gun on your uncle."

"You mean it's all right?" I asked, wrinkling my forehead so that she could see I didn't quite understand.

"Of course not," she said. "You don't feel all right, do you?"

"No, ma'am," I said. "I don't think I could ever forget the look on Dunstan's face."

"Your Uncle Willie would have liked to hear that," she told me, looking away.

"I wish I could tell him, Mama. I wish I could thank him. There's so much inside me I never got to tell him."

"He knew," she said. "Eric, you never in your life kept any part of you hidden. Your whole life is written in those sad eyes of yours. He knew how you felt, that's for sure."

I tried to believe that, but as the days passed, a frown was my most constant companion. I tended the feed store and checked the fences. I did my chores, swam with my brothers in the creek, even helped Mama put a fresh coat of paint on the house. I carved his name on the cross. But now there was no warmth, no laughter in my life.

I watched the way Tom and Willie ran across the fields, laughed and splashed in the creek. I was jealous of the life they'd found, the joy that filled their moments. I wanted so very much to be my old self again, the boy who'd ridden with his father to see a herd of buffalo.

One afternoon as Tom and I were checking the fences, we came across a place where the wire had been pulled away from the posts. I climbed down from my horse and pulled out my hammer. As I worked on the wires, sweat poured down my forehead, stinging my eyes. I was tired and hot. Even Tom's jokes failed to brighten my mood.

"It'll sure feel good to dump myself in the creek today," Tom said. "August just gets hotter."

"Yeah," I said, wiping the sweat from my face. "It'll cool off in a few weeks."

"Then comes school. Winter after that. It's going to be lonesome this Christmas without Papa," Tom said, staring at me.

"I expect," I said.

I took the hammer and nailed the barbed wire back to the fenceposts. I was glad of the noise. I didn't feel like talking anymore just then. When I finally finished, I put the hammer in my saddlebag and motioned to Tom to mount up.

"I sure hope the creek's cold today," Tom said, taking off his shirt and wringing out the perspiration.

"Willie'll be waiting," I said.

"Then let's ride," Tom said, spurring his horse.

We raced off through a ravine and across the flat cow pastures. As we passed the little cemetery on the hill, I pulled up my horse.

"Hey, aren't you coming?" Tom asked.

"Later," I said to him. "I've got something to do."

"Don't take too long," Tom said. "We'll use up all the water."

I didn't respond to Tom's joke. As he disappeared from my sight, I slid down from the saddle, leaving the reins to dangle at my horse's side. Standing beside the simple white crosses, I looked at the names. John Sheidler the first read. Behind it were the other two old ones. Elsa Sheidler, Michael Sheidler they said. Then there was the new one, the one with the fresh coat of white paint. On it was carved William Delamer III.

"I didn't mean for you to die, Uncle Willie," I said, kneeling beside the fence. "I wanted you to come back and live with us. I thought maybe you'd like to take Papa's place. I figured you could teach me what a man's got to know."

I stopped talking long enough to rub the tears from my eyes.

"Mama and the reverend say maybe you've finally found peace. I don't really understand what kind of peace they're talking about. I know about the kind of peace you find when the moon's bright and the night's still. It makes me feel good, kind of close to God. I hope that's what Mama meant, 'cause it's what I'd like you to have."

I stepped over the small fence and felt the side of the simple wooden cross. Then I looked to Papa's grave and took a deep breath, blinking away the tears rolling down my cheeks.

"Papa, I'll tend to things," I said softly. "I'm a man now, and I can do what's got to be done."

I wiped my eyes and backed away from the

graves. Then I stepped over the little fence made so long ago by a man now dead and a boy now different. Another step and I was to my horse. Then I grabbed the saddlehorn and pulled myself up on top of the horse.

"Good-bye, Papa, Uncle Willie, Michael, Elsa," I said, feeling the tears roll down my cheeks and fall to my chest.

I turned my horse away from the graveyard and headed for the creek. Tom and Willie would be splashing in the water, and soon I would be with them. It would be a different me, though. Just as the jagged scar on my shoulder made me seem older, less of a boy, so it was that the scar on my heart changed me also.

When I reached the creek, the wind swept away the last tear I would shed for Uncle Willie or myself. I left behind what had been and walked forward into an uncertain future. It was a better, brighter me that stepped down from my horse. And on my face was the first smile of many that would come in the days ahead.

THE NEWEST ADVENTURES AND ESCAPADES OF BOLT
by Cort Martin